I0522939

VAN CORTLANDT PARK

VAN CORTLANDT PARK

DON KELLIN

Copyright © 2022 Don Kellin

All rights reserved. No part of this book may be reproduced or transmitted in any form or by any means, electronic or mechanical, including photocopying, recording, or by any information storage and retrieval system, except in the case of brief quotations embodied in critical articles and reviews, without prior written permission of the publisher.

Paperback ISBN: 978-0-9896170-2-4
eBook ISBN: 978-0-9896170-3-1

Printed in the United States of America

Cover and Interior Design: Creative Publishing Book Design

CHAPTER 1

The painted lady, her back to the boardwalk, stood there ankle deep in the Atlantic gazing east through her false lashes toward the land of her ancestors and unpainted past.

Only budget-conscious regulars, male and female, had spent any time with her, under the boardwalk, in dark doorways, across the towel-covered back seats of cars, or for an extra twenty bucks, on the sliver of mattress that never had time to relax and flatten out completely once pulled from the bowels of the worn tweed-covered sofa convertible opposite her sacrosanct bed, both furnishings provided by Rockaway's only apartment hotel, The Palace, a five-story brick cube surrounded by clapboard bungalows.

Facing the massive August moon laying down a shimmering path across the black sea to her ankles, the painted lady scrubbed away her painted face, the last four hours, the last three years. Her lips were pink again, the face was her face.

She looked down at the lashes spinning on the silver foam eroding her foot prints and spoke to them. "You'll be gone in a few minutes – and so will I. I've had enough of you – and this world – and me."

The painted lady clenched her jaw, breathed deeply, clutched the worn azure cameo pendant nestled between her breasts and started toward the slivers of iridescent whitecaps, the breakers and the unknown.

CHAPTER 2

A hundred yards behind second base, past the ratty outfield's clumps of alchemy that turned rollers into mini pop-ups, in a small clearing buried in a thicket of bushes, saplings and their ancestors, the pasty old man failed his second attempt to fall asleep. His first attempt had been made where it always was, a few blocks away on the folding cot in the eight by ten windowless cinder-block drywall cube, a corner build-out in the basement of the six-story fifty-year-old apartment building that Mr. Nowicki, the Polish building superintendent, had leased to him in 1953 for $100 a month rent cash under the table, for the last twenty years. Priscilla Cates, the owner of the building, willed to her by Murray Cates, nee Katz, her deceased, almost Jewish slumlord father, was born, raised and spoiled-rotten on Long Island in the post-prime Southampton mansion she still lived in. The other buildings her father had owned had long since crumbled to their lots now covered with chunks of mortar, brick dust, unpaid property taxes – and a history no one in the neighborhood knew or cared about – and neither did Priscilla Cates. She did, however, care that her loving father hadn't paid property taxes for eight years and forgot to tell his co-owner daughter that she was saddled with debt before he jetted down to oblivion. And so the slumlord's daughter, her Haitian servant, Cecilia Papouloute, and the Southampton mansion were totally dependent on the rents from the apartment building her father had built in 1922 and on Mr. Nowicki, the building's Polish über-super who made sure rents were paid on time and the building was maintained like none other in the neighborhood. Murray Cates had made sure his "flagship" building belonged in the upscale North Bronx and was worthy of the partial view of Van Cortlandt Park. Unlike the typical slum tenements he had collected over the years, his pride and joy was six stories and had an Otis elevator, servicing each of the two identical wings that had six identical apartments a floor. Every unit had a bath shower combination and windows in the bedrooms. The queue for a vacant apartment could have wrapped around the block, but there was never a vacancy for more time than it took for the paramedics to leave the building. As for Izolda Nowicki, the super's wife, on her wedding night shortly after she arrived from Poland, the man who was the family's consensus choice to be her life mate, cautioned her that everything would be fine as long as she minded her own business and prepared his meals from his mother's recipes.

Shortly after the old man moved into the cube, a tenant seeking to gain favor, managed to reach Priscilla Cates and tell her about the old man and her suspicions that Nowicki was on the take. What the whistleblower didn't know was that Murray Cates's daughter not only knew about the old man, she also knew Nowicki was skimming from the basement's six coin-operated washing machines and dryers, in constant use by the building's seventy tenants – and that confronting him wasn't an option. The idea of spending time in the Bronx interviewing a new super was repulsive. At least Nowicki's "tenants" was Jewish. Her father had taught her that Jewish tenants are clean and always pay their rent on time. In fact, lying there in the Montefiore Medical Center, the last few words Murray Cates gasped while squeezing his daughter's aching knuckles were, "Rent to Jews even though they're a pain in the ass."

As long as Nowicki was getting away with embezzling the old man's rent and skimming coins at will, Priscilla Cates was pretty certain he and his wife, Izolda would be there forever and never ask for anything. Asking for anything never crossed the über-super's mind. Thus, his employer made believe she didn't know, and Nowicki made believe he didn't know she was making believe she didn't know.

Between back property taxes, interest, insurance and maintenance, Murray Cates's daughter was barely breaking even, and although the eggs she was walking on were hard boiled, another straw or two could break them and her back.

As for the whistleblower, her son had long since moved his mother to Miami to make sure she was as far south as possible and would spend her ten-carat gold-filled golden years surrounded by purple coifs, early bird specials and people who looked and sounded like her.

CHAPTER 3

In the first few years tenants had offered the old man food, clothes and conversation, but he turned his back on them and walked away. The few children in the building, cautioned to disregard the specter in the basement, couldn't resist trying to catch a glimpse from time to time. The building hummed along, planted securely on the whites-only oasis of the North Bronx until Izolda Nowicki, while her spouse was off hunting with buddies, signed up her first rental after hearing the applicant's story while looking at his beautiful Puerto Rican family. To Umberto Ruiz, the neighborhood and building were Shangri-la, the reward for decades of struggle to make sure that he and his family escaped Bayamon, Puerto Rico, East Harlem and finally join uptown's middle class. The super's wife found the family irresistible. As the ink dried, Umberto Ruiz, his wife, Motita and their 15 year-old daughter, Rita, became the first Puerto Rican family in the neighborhood.

Mr. Nowicki returned a few days later with a chest freezer's worth of innocent flesh and bone and a less than impressive set of antlers to grace their living room wall, tangible proof that he was a man's man, but the length of his penis was probably closer to five inches than six.

He was shocked and incensed at what she had done and raised his hand to teach her a lesson then lowered it when she threatened to close the amusement park between her legs if her husband touched her or voided the lease.

To Nowicki, the rental was a palpable threat to his dominance. To his wife, it was proof she might be underestimating the strength of her spine and will. To the tenants, it was the beginning of the end.

The old man's rent included a 3-inch nail in the wall, a night stand family vultures left behind after they emptied apartments of their deceased grandma's treasures and a folding cot and striped mattress he couldn't take his eyes off as he changed the sheet every other day. Over the years, he had seen a plain cot mattress or two leaning against alley walls or lying in repose on some pile of garbage much like he could have ended up if it weren't for cowardice, courage or something else he couldn't put his finger on. A few summer mornings in the park, gazing up at the canopy of leaves and the wrens going about their business, he thought he understood – but not for long. On some clear summer nights, wearing the faded black vest he never took off, he would lie on his blue tarp gazing up through the blackness at stars, not certain they still existed. He felt the same way about his image reflected in the rust-speckled mirrored door that clung to the rusted metal cabinet that clung to a piece of drywall nailed between two studs above a stained porcelain sink that hadn't felt the comfort of warm water since it was deemed too small for the basement's utility sink and was dislodged and moved from its home opposite the washing machines. The sort-of-a-bathroom had a stained toilet, an overhead tank and chain and a sort of dry-walled shower enclosure that was slapped together to placate the last in the line of supers who almost melted while feeding the building's antique coal furnace during the winter. When the old man took a shower, so did everything within six feet including the drywall that was misnamed.

***

The Nowicki's moved into a larger first floor apartment just after the building's new electronic furnace was installed. Murray Cates's accountant had finally provided incontrovertible proof that a modern building heater would save his frugal client money in the long run. Turns out he was right – but Murray Cates had had a short run. He was probably pissed off wherever he had landed.

During winters, the deposed coal furnace had provided some ambient heat in the basement. The new furnace only provided some strange clicking noises. For the first five years of its reign, on some winter days and most winter nights, the old man relied on heat radiating from the busy washers and dryers. When they were resting in the middle of night, layers of blankets, a ratty fur hat and a few scarves helped some, but when they failed to he would spend the night sitting against one of the dryers he roused from slumber.

CHAPTER 4

In year three of his tenancy, Izolda Nowicki, after being stunned into sobbing by a PBS special on the Krakow ghetto, had plowed through her husband's "leave well enough alones" and paperwork and found the old man's application. All it had was his scribbled, illegible name, the name and address of his only employer for decades, Berkowitz Furrier on Twenty-Ninth Street in Manhattan, his Jewish ethnicity, and the place of his birth, Krakow, Poland. The revelation sent her to the bedroom. She lay there buried under the realization that while she was jumping rope during her oblivious, pre-teen life, the Jews were being hunted like rabid dogs and living, starving and dying as sub-humans a few feet away behind a wall her father probably supplied and laid some of the bricks for.

She cajoled her husband into teaching the Jew the string-coin-box-hack that rendered the coin boxes helpless and the use of the washers and dryers gratis. He resisted until she shared her premonition that she would be getting headaches every time he wanted her.

The old man used the machines constantly because he owned only one sheet, one pillow case, two tank undershirts, a New York Yankee T-shirt, two pairs of jockey shorts, two pair of lisle hose and two white never-press Dacron shirts. The rest of his wardrobe consisted of two pairs of shiny black gabardine pants, one belt, two pairs of Keds high tops, one white, one black, a jacket, over coat and the vest as worn and frayed as the man who wore them. A neatly folded blue plastic tarp that doubled as a rain poncho and a ground cover rested on a discarded night table he had found in the alley.

In year four, Izolda, again not heeding the advice of her husband, tried to connect with the old man, but he would have none of it and didn't utter a word.

"I told you so," asserted Mr. Nowicki. "I know what's best."

"For who? Who is it best for?" his irritated wife asked.

She thought she was better-prepared, pad and pencil in hand standing at his door, a few weeks later.

"Because I'm also from Krakow, and I want my husband to make a mail box for you so you won't have to go to Arthur Avenue to pick up your new social security checks."

He gently closed the door while she stood there.

CHAPTER 5

The old man's $600 social security check was the return for the deduction taken from his weekly paycheck for twenty of the 25 years he combed out staples from stretched, dried fur pelts. In year twenty-one, his appreciative boss, Berkowitz, decided, unilaterally, to pay the man who never asked him for anything, cash under the table so he would be eligible to collect full social security. The combined income was more than his favorite employee felt he deserved. From it, he took only what he needed to survive. The balance was kept in a locked, gutted circuit breaker box not because he ever intended to use it, but because throughout his childhood, while the Krakow sun shone down on his family, his mama and papa had taught him to save. He was a good son and a whiz at sourcing goods and negotiating the buy price for just about anything to do with the jewelry shop he would inherit someday. He had a beautiful voice and would sing for neighbors and customers in the store. He listened, learned and was far from stubborn except for one thing—he was determined to marry for love unlike his parents who fell in love years after their wedding.

He preferred looking for a mate in a haystack to eliminating his parents fear that they would not have grandchildren. Year after year they, their neighbors and a multitude of customers who frequented the family's popular jewelry store paraded an assortment of prospects all of whom were gently rejected. At the end of January 1936, at the age of thirty, God rewarded him and his family with Ruth, a 23-year-old beauty he had fallen head over heels in love with. The angel, Rachel, a product of that love, was born a year later. Bathed in a sea of love, surrounded by swarms of unsettling rumors and uncertainty, Rachel, the angel, fell asleep every night to the sweet tenor voice of her father singing the melodic, *Oyfin Pripetchik*, the most popular Yiddish bedtime lullaby.

His father incessantly urged the couple to save their Zloty for a rainy day because he knew the Jew-hating Austrian upstart who had eroded faith in his own country's democracy wouldn't stop at the border. Fear became reality and the rain started. Poland was invaded, and by 1940 tens of thousands of Jews had already left Kazimierz, their Jewish community, for who knew where. Nazi officers who frequented their shop looking for gifts for their wives and mistresses were acting like partners, and Jews were being purged from institutions and forced to wear yellow stars on their outer garments.

And then it rained harder –much harder – and money was useless. More than 30 years later, it still was.

CHAPTER 6

Standing in his doorway, this time Izolda Nowicki persisted with passion.

"Stop being stubborn! If you have a mailbox you won't have to take the two buses back and forth to Arthur Avenue for your check every month. And who knows what other benefit you might get? There's no paperwork on you. Just print your name so I can read it."

She studied his face, explored his faded blue eyes. He reached for the pad and pencil. She looked down at the terrible scars all over his knuckles and the three rows of tattoos, one above the other, on his right forearm five inches above his wrist. The first was 201989, below was 202192 and below that was 202266. She tried to memorize them, but he looked up, saw her transfixed, quickly withdrew his hands, turned and headed for his bed. She stood there hands still extended, a pencil in one, a yellow pad in the other. Another failure. Izolda Nowicki wanted desperately to know more about him and the dark times even though she knew that going down that path might lead to a minefield, or even worse, to quicksand, but she had no choice.

The following day, she told her busy husband she was bored, and he suggested she should take up hiking around the park. And so he was pleased his stubborn wife was hiking around the enormous park for hours every day while she sat pouring through everything she could lay her hands on about the Holocaust at the New York Public Library in Riverdale and on 42nd Street. Rather than spending the rest of her childless-life cooking, cleaning and lying under her husband until he was finished, she had decided deciphering the old man would be her life's work.

She resisted sharing her burgeoning knowledge with and asking questions of the old man, but did make her husband cut down the top of his door and add a transom so he could get some air without leaving his door open. The occasional breeze created by the open transom and cellar door provided some relief, but on very hot nights he continued to sleep in the park.

CHAPTER 7

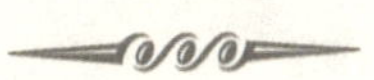

Her eyes squinted open, as the rising sun escaped the horizon and slowly painted her face with light as she lay there on the wooden slats of the boardwalk bench. She ran her hands over her torso then grabbed the collars of the coat she was wrapped in and pulled them tight around her neck. A wave of disappointment was all she felt except for the hand on her forehead and the lap that cradled the nape of her neck. She tried and failed to raise her head before she spoke without opening her eyes.

"What were you doing on the beach at two in the morning?"

"I haven't been sleeping lately," a man's voice answered.

"Do I know you?"

"Not personally."

"Why didn't you let me go?"

"Because after my Silvia died, I got as far out as you did."

CHAPTER 8

Rita Ruiz's pleas not to be torn away from dozens of lifelong friendships with her own kind hadn't made a dent in her father's decision to move uptown. Sermons about being a pioneer and setting an example in an alien, lily-white neighborhood hadn't resonated. All the stories about how Roberto Clemente, born in his hometown of Carolina, Puerto Rico, had endured the taunts and indignations on the way to baseball's Hall of Fame hadn't helped as she walked the gauntlet of epithets and slurs in the hallways and dodged even worse as she traversed the schoolyard of her new lily-white school.

Once again she dragged her morbid demeanor across the street to her refuge, stepped onto the grass pounding the pocket of her baseball mitt with her fist, thankful for the few boy-players who seemed to tolerate her and throw her the ball once in a while. She paused, looked up, breathed in the difference between the aroma of pastilles and arroz con pollo that permeated the East Harlem air and the alien scents of Van Cortlandt Park. Then, rather than walk around the block to home plate, she opted for a short cut through the thicket of bushes that ringed the outfield and almost tripped over the old man lying there in the casket-sized clearing, flat on his back, mouth open, head resting on the vest-covered surface root of an elm. She stood there for a moment sorting out what she was looking at, dropped to her knees, saw the three rows of tattoos, then moved closer to check if he was breathing.

"Go away!" he yelled at the ear inches from his mouth.

Startled, she rocketed backwards against the sharp, bone-hard tips of branches and screamed.

"Jesus Christ, you scared the shit out of me!"

He peered at her without saying anything.

She freed her impaled T-shirt from the branches, sat up and stared at him.

"I thought you were dead."

"Go and leave me alone," he pleaded.

"You're the spook in the basement, aren't you?"

"Just go away."

"My name is Rita Ruiz."

"We just moved in a month ago."

"Why do you live this way?"

"Why don't you say something?"

She rose, looked down at him. "What is it with you idiots up here?" she exploded. "Especially you!" She pointed to the numbers on his arm. "My class just studied the holocaust. My mother cried when she read my school book."

The old man sat up, said nothing.

Rita shook her head.

"Haven't you seen enough of hatred and disrespect?"

"Go away!" the old man shouted.

"Damn it, old man! How can you be like the rest of them up here! I hate this place and I hate you. Fuck off!"

She bolted through a narrow clearing, leaving shards of her tee shirt behind and emerged on the grass of center field looking for someone, anyone to have a catch with.

CHAPTER 9

Two streets away from the Nowicki fief, a new apartment building became the first in the neighborhood to boast central air conditioning. Central air was never an option for Murray Cates. Even if there had been space for ducts and a roof that could bear the weight of the condensers, he couldn't bear the thought of an unnecessary expenditure tampering with the bottom line of his cash cow in Riverdale. If challenged, Priscilla Cates' father would have suggested tenant's buy better fans and wear lighter tops to avoid melting in their apartments. Cash poor Priscilla Cates, totally reliant on a few annuities to keep up with day to day necessities but not the Jones's, convinced by her über-super that if nothing was done about the heat there would be a rent strike and some tenants might leave if she didn't do something, cashed in the last of the savings bonds left to her by her debt-compromised daddy to update the building's electrical capacity to accommodate the extra load necessary to juice window air conditioners. Some tenants bought the new Carrier window unit. Some tenants didn't. Several tenants left to move into the new apartment building that featured central air and apartment thermostats, planting seeds of doubt about the future of the Cates' cash cow in everyone except Priscilla Cates, who was too occupied doing nothing to notice.

Nowicki installed the units the tenants opted to buy. The ten bucks per installation he charged, the tips he received more often than not, the commission from Carrier for each unit, the skimmed cash and the old man's rent kept Nowicki's micro-conglomerate stable and producing more revenue than his salary.

The window unit in the Nowicki bedroom provided plenty of cool air. It also provided plenty of buzzing noises because the man Izolda shared her bed with, the almost handy man, botched the installation and was too busy wedging and shimming dozens of his other botched installations to fix his own. Except on rare occasions, her husband's snoring and the air conditioner's symphony usurped the possibility of thought, contemplation or sleep. Not so on this night. There was neither buzzing nor snoring. And so Izolda Nowicki's head was resting on her pillow not under it.

Does he have a family of any kind anywhere? Why is he living like he lives? thirty years from the camps and he still lives like a prisoner. Why does he behave the way he does? There has to be reason for all of this.

During the same night, a night still heated by the sun that had melted into it, the transom provided no relief. Again the old man donned his vest, ran his fingers the bumpy length of its hem and headed for the park while the super's wife poured over her collection of library books about the Holocaust.

CHAPTER 10

Nor'easters, hurricanes, off season, on season, the tiny Moe's Bagels had been there for the painted lady at six every morning so she could fill the void with a gratis day-old cinnamon raison bagel smothered with lox cream cheese and a cup of coffee before she returned to her sacrosanct bed and slept the day away. Diego had served her every morning during his mini-break after removing the day's kneaded bagel dough from the spiral mixer. Rumpelstiltskin had bestowed the miller's daughter with the magic to spin straw into gold. Moe, in addition to teaching Diego how to say a "gut'n morg'n," "zeyn gezunt" and "gotenyu," had bestowed his right-hand man with the magic to spin and shape the proprietary dough mixture into something more valuable than gold. Lox and cream cheese are useless on a gold bagel. Moe had also insisted he stay in college instead of banking his future on when and if his boss would retire and leave the shop minus a payout to his trusted employee.

"Making a life is not waiting for things out of your control," Moe advised. "When you get out of bed you go for it not wait for it."

Queens College was free and Moe took care of books and assorted fees.

Life was good, but it would have been better if Alphonso Israel, the ancient Puerto Rican who owned the shop next to him, would retire and cease making luscious rotisserie chickens whose skins looked exactly like his after they were plucked. They slowly rotated on spits hugging the window, and every day every single one of them would end up hugging the linings of the intestines of smiling patrons. The name, ISRAEL'S CHICKENS, on the window guaranteed "the chosen ones" and gentiles alike would gobble up the chickens and make his mattress lumpier. He closed his shop when the last chicken flapped adios. No one knew when that would be. He didn't deliver or reserve chickens in any amount. He also didn't accept checks or credit cards. If you wanted a lot of chickens, getting there early with enough cash helped your odds. The entire neighborhood debated what he was worth, but only his mattress knew. Moe's Bagels had four tables and a narrow, six-foot space between them and the counter. Moe offered Al the moon for the space over and over again, but the chicken man demurred.

During the summer, when his shop was busy, Moe would count the number of potential customers who peeled off the queue outside his door. In the winter it was worse. They didn't even make the trip. Moe dreamed of the potential El Dorado next door – Forty more square feet of cooking space, ten tables for four with waitress service, an air conditioned oasis in the summer and a warm refuge in the winter. He wished no harm on his neighbor. However, he never hesitated to ask how his neighbor was feeling.

"How are you today?" Moe would ask.

"My doctor told me to tell you to be patient," he would answer.

CHAPTER 11

With the crowds gone, Moe had started coming in at 6:30 but not that morning. The bagel baker and painted lady had arrived at the front door at three. He placed his shoulder against her exhausted body, pinning her limp torso to the door jam while he brushed the sand from her feet then opened the door. He brought her into the stockroom and set her down on the mattress he often slept on after his wife died and his attempts to fall asleep in the bed they had shared for a lifetime had failed. He surrounded her with bags of flour to block the draft pouring into the space between the bottom of alley door and the concrete floor. He lingered a bit then lied down next to her, and as he closed his eyes he murmured, "Sweetheart, don't be jealous. How I wish it was you next to me."

He woke a few hours later. She wasn't there. He rushed into the shop and found her sitting at the rear table, her head resting on it.

He sat opposite her for a while trying to sort out what could have driven this beautiful woman to end up in her hell.

She finally raised her head and moaned.

"Are you the one who did this to me?"

"Did this to you?" he asked.

He tilted his head and gazed at her face. He had never seen it unpainted.

"Do you know how beautiful you are?"

"I'm none of your business."

"Do you? Do you know what a beautiful woman you are?"

"It'll still cost you $25."

"Why should you talk to me that way?"

"I told you that I'm none of your business."

"But you are. You're in my business every day. Mind you, it's not my most profitable relationship, and I gag when I think of lox and cream cheese on a raisin cinnamon bagel, but I like the idea that someone needs my place, my bagels and maybe, someday, even me."

She rested her head on the table again and was fast asleep in a few seconds.

CHAPTER 12

The old man sat at the edge of the cot wiping the sweat from his neck and forehead. He lifted himself up and grabbed his vest and tarp. On the floor above, Izolda had put her books under the bed and tried to sleep, but when she closed her eyes the same gaunt faces and sunken eyes of the young girls reaching out to her had made sleep impossible. She slipped out of bed, left the bedroom, made a cup of tea, and sat by the living room window gazing down at the dimly-lit empty street. The old man emerged from the building's side alley carrying a tarp. He crossed the street and headed toward the park. The super's wife jumped into a pair of dungarees threw on a blouse, slid into flip flops, made sure her husband was sleeping. She didn't make a sound as she left the apartment and rushed out into the street and the hot, viscous August air. She raced to the corner, looked around and caught a glimpse of the old man disappearing into the tall bushes that surrounded the park.

She hurried across the street, slowed down when she hit the grass and stopped at the bushes. She hesitated but had no choice. The old man put down the tarp and leaned back against his tree waiting to see who or what was approaching him through the thicket at three in the morning. First were the fingers spreading a crevice through the branches, then the arms, then his landlord's wife. They stared at each other. She fidgeted, then spoke.

"I've been reading about those times. I've been reading every day. When I can sleep, I dream about what you went through. Don't you want someone you can talk to, spend some time with?"

He didn't respond.

"We don't have to talk about back then."

He reached down for the tarp, grabbed it up and yelled at her.

"Just like that you push yourself on me, and it doesn't bother you that I don't want someone to talk to or someone to spend time with! Would I live like I do if I wanted to spend time with you or anyone!?

A moment passed.

"Thank you for what you do for me, but I'm telling you, I'll find another basement or live in the park if you don't mind your own business!"

"I feel terrible," she said.

"Go to a doctor."

"Haven't I been good to you? I haven't bothered you except to try to make your life a little easier. Please help me."

"Help you? Help you with what?" he reacted.

"Help me to sleep at night."

"What?"

"I'm having great difficulty."

"With me? With what?"

Izolda Nowicki fell to her knees and started to sob.

"Why are you crying?

She raised her head, wiped her eyes. "I grew up in Krakow. My father was a bricklayer. He worked on that wall while I played a few feet from it. I played a few feet from you, not a worry in the world. I played while you and your family—"

"It's not your business! You did nothing wrong. You were only a child. Enough already! I can't help you. Go back to your husband and leave me alone!"

He headed into the bushes.

She yelled out to him, "Tell me why you have all that writing on your arm? I went to the library and read and looked at lists and photographs. No one has tattoos like yours."

The old man disappeared through the bushes. The super's wife, still on her knees, stared forwarded trying to figure out her next move.

CHAPTER 13

As usual, Diego showed up at 4 a.m. He opened the alley door, started in and tripped over a bag of flour. After the bags were stacked where they belonged, he opened the door to the store and saw the odd couple. Moe signaled no talking with his forefinger across his lips. His right hand man nodded okay, did an about face, returned to the store-room and began to work. Two hours later, Diego watched the odd couple from behind the counter while he spooned out creamed pickled herring from a large jar into a stainless steel tray, then placed it alongside the other trays in the refrigerated display case. He wiped his hands on the apron tied around his waist, came out from behind the counter and approached the table. Moe shrugged he didn't know what to do next.

Diego bent down until he was looking at her face, his temple on the table. He whispered to her seductively.

"Tu desayuno es listo mi amor."

"Diego, you shouldn't talk to her that way," scolded Moe.

"Jefe," Diego shot back. "All I said was 'your breakfast is ready, my love.' I always call her my love. It makes her smile."

Moe hesitated, then, "Did you? Did you ever? Did you ever—"

"Did I ever what?" reacted Diego.

"You know what."

"Christ, you know me since I was in my stroller salivating opposite your chocolate chip bagels. Gotenyu, Moe!"

She opened her eyes and murmured, "Por favor, déjeme en paz."

"Well then," squinted Moe. "How did you know she speaks Spanish?"

"We only speak in Spanish."

"Is she Puerto Rican?"

"Jefe, a few dozen people who aren't Puerto Rican also speak Spanish."

"How do you say, don't be a wise ass in Spanish?

"Eres una persona maravillosa," answered Diego. "And she's from Argentina, from a town called Bariloche. But her parents moved to Mendoza when she was about four."

Moe rose. "Maybe a cup of coffee under her nose will get her attention.

"Black. Five sugars," she murmured, as she raised her head off the table

CHAPTER 14

The sun's rays, horizontal at sun up, skipped off the damp asphalt paths that crisscrossed the park's dew covered grass; silver ribbons over shiny green gift-wrap. As the sun rose above tree level, a wave of sunlight flooded the east west canyons formed by the apartment buildings lining the streets of Riverdale.

Izolda Nowicki lifted her shopping cart over the doorway saddle of the pristine deco building's humongous wrought iron-framed glass door to the street and found Rita Ruiz, lost in thought, sitting on the front steps. She placed her cart on the sidewalk, returned up the few steps and sat next to her.

"Hi," she said.

"Buenos dios," Rita responded.

"You're parents seem very nice."

No response.

Have you made many friends yet?

"Hundreds."

"That bad, huh,"

"What do you think?"

"Young lady when I came to America, I went to my aunt and uncle in Brooklyn. They live in Greenpoint. My uncle makes shoes and my aunt puts collars on shirts in Long Island City. I learned English in high school, but everyone in the neighborhood spoke Polish. You didn't have to know English except when you went to the movies. I learned more English at the movies than in school."

"Why are you telling me this?"

"I'm just trying to make conversation."

"Conversation? They have conversations in Riverdale? I thought they were illegal."

"These people didn't have much to say to me either after my husband dragged me away from my friends and family to take the job here. After a few months I was so sad my teacher made me sit down, took a book from her draw, opened it, handed it to me. She asked me to read the words she pointed to. It was written by a Greek philosopher named Epictetus.

"It's not what happens to you, but how you react to it that matters," read Izolda.

"The people up here suck," moaned Rita.

"I agree, but that's not a reason to spend your own life being miserable."

"One of the kids in my history class asked our teacher if she knew why there's a war going on somewhere every day year after year."

"Did she have an answer?"

"Not really."

"Do you?"

"It's beautiful up here but the people aren't. They blame everyone and everything for being so damn miserable instead of looking in the mirror."

"That's a very special answer from a very special young lady. You have to share that with Epictetus."

"He's another one who doesn't talk to me."

Izolda put her arm around Rita. "Well, I'm talking to you. May I call you Rita?"

"That's my name."

"Have you ever had a Polish friend?"

"No."

"Then I'll be your first Polish friend if you'll be my first Puerto Rican friend, and please call me Izolda."

"Izolda?" reacted Rita.

"I didn't choose it."

"I have a friend named Isabella. We call her Izzie."

"So call me Izzie too. I like it. What should we talk about, Rita? What interests you?"

"The old man interests me. I want to talk about the old man."

"He's Polish like me," said Izolda.

"So was Chopin and Copernicus." said Rita. "But they didn't live in a basement and bushes. What's wrong with him? Why is he like he is? Why do you let him stay here?"

"He pays rent like everyone else."

"Why does he live like he does?"

"He's been through a lot."

"That's no excuse. If all the Negroes, Latinos and Jews acted like him we'd be living in hell."

"He has lived in hell."

"It's all so complicated," moaned Rita. "Does he work?"

"Almost thirty years in the same place."

"He told you all that?"

"Mr. Nowicki checked it out before renting to him."

He still works most days even though he collects social security."

"What does he do?"

"He works for a company that makes fur coats. I don't know what he did years ago, but now he uses a metal comb to remove the staples from fur skins that were soaked in water, stretched and stapled to a big plywood board. He has scars from the staples all over his knuckles."

I saw the scars," said Rita. "I thought the Nazis tortured him. He actually had a conversation with you?"

"No. I followed him downtown last week and watched him work. He's no different there. He speaks to no one."

A moment passed.

"Y ahora que? So what now?" asked Rita.

"Utopiamy go w życzliwości."

"You must be kidding," said Rita.

"We drown him in kindness," answered her new buddy.

CHAPTER 15

Another first day of the month and the same rendezvous. Once again, the old man took the empty, graffiti-splattered Broadway Seventh Avenue Line rumbling and squealing its way under Manhattan from Van Cortlandt Park to Battery Park. As usual, he boarded the first ferry to her at 8:30 a.m.. He took his spot at the tip of the prow gazed out to sea and then at her. Her patina had darkened, but not her attitude. He walked down the boat ramp and to his usual spot on the bench opposite her base.

Once again he read the inscription and could hear her speaking. "Give me your tired," she said, and he was so tired. "Give me your poor," and he might as well have been. But none of her words described what he had become better than "wretched refuse."

His trysts with the lady, his trusted confidant, a lady he could talk to, a relationship with the only woman left in his life, was coming to an end. It was taking longer to escape his aches and pains in the morning and become mobile. Taking a later ferry was out of the question. By ten o'clock, the ferries were packed and the island was no longer theirs.

CHAPTER 16

The painted lady chose to walk back to her room along Seagirt Boulevard instead of the boardwalk even though she had 'serviced' many bus drivers parked on that boulevard while their buses were 'out of service.' Feeling unsteady, she had barely resisted Moe's insistence that he walk her home certain that not even steady customers would recognize her without paint.

"We could have walked along the boardwalk," he said. "We could have," she responded. "I spend more time under it than on it."

"Those days are over young lady."

"What makes you think so?"

"When Diego started Queens College we made an arrangement. He comes in at 4 a.m. and leaves at noon. He also works a full day on Saturday, and Sunday is for homework unless he wants to put in a few hours for an extra few bucks and his grades are B or better. So, you'll work from noon to four during the week and on the weekends from seven to three or four. When the summer starts and the bungalows fill up we stay open until seven and that means more money. Also, there's me. I'd like some time off to smell the roses instead of yeast. The job pays five dollars an hour and comes with bagel benefits. Someday you and Diego might end up with this place for a few bucks if you send me enough money for suntan lotion and fishing stuff."

"You're so sure of yourself," said Anna.

"I'm surer of you."

"You don't know who I am or what I am."

"I do know who you are and what you are. Now I want to know who you were and what you were and what you're going to be. Let's go to the boardwalk and sit for a while," said Moe rubbing the small of his back with the heels of his hands.

She didn't respond.

"Lady, you owe it to me. I carried you most of the way back to the shop. I almost slipped a disc."

CHAPTER 17

Rita and Izolda couldn't set their bedside alarm clocks because there would be no reasonable explanation for doing so. Sleep wasn't an option. They waited on the front step and took turns peeking around the corner of the building's front entry alcove. At 6:30, Rita saw him appear from the alley. When he turned the corner on the way to the subway they rushed into the tunnel toward the rear of the building, across the concrete courtyard and into the door to the street-level basement and the cubicle. They opened the unpainted ¾ inch plywood door and entered the old man's space. The closet was the three-inch nail in drywall with a coat, a sweater and a pair of pants on wire hangers hung from it. A night table with two drawers and a lamp with a bulb but no shade abutted a cot with a pillow and cover neatly folded at the foot of the bed. The only other things in the room were a pair of Keds on the floor under the 'closet and a frayed extension cord from the lamp through a hole in the drywall that led to an outlet somewhere. Rita went to the night table and gingerly opened the top drawer. A half-empty box of quart-sized Ziplocs, a pair of neatly folded lisle socks, a pair of Jockey shorts, a T-shirt, and a handkerchief were all she found.

In the second drawer were a few subway tokens, a pencil, and when she ran her hand along the backside of the drawer she felt three flat objects. She carefully slid them forward. One was a scrap of paper with three double digits penciled on it. The other two were envelopes. The flap glue on the smaller envelope was yellowed and brittle and no longer sealed the contents. The larger envelope flap was glued tight. She held it in front of the lamp. They looked like documents but were unreadable. As she lifted the smaller one to place it on the top of the table, tiny shards of dried glue were dislodged and fell back into the drawer and onto the table top. She gently wedged her thumbnail under the envelope flap, lifted it and slid the contents out. There were only two faded sepia photographs next to each other in a plastic sleeve. Rita turned on the lamp. They peered at the photographs through the foggy plastic afraid that if they removed them they might be marred.

The first was an image of an older couple. The man wore a wide-lapelled double breasted suit, a long-collared shirt, a short, wide foulard tie with a perfect Windsor knot and a smile beaming brightly enough to light the draw when it was closed. The woman at his side gazed down at the swaddled baby cradled against her breast. A young woman stood next to them facing the camera, holding the handle of a baby carriage. They were posing on a street corner under a street sign that was barely legible. The second photograph was of a young couple holding the hands of a dressed up two or three year-old girl. An empty stroller stood between them and the same man and woman who were in the other photograph. He had not stopped beaming. They were posing in front of a store. The burnished gold letters forming an arch across the store window said:

Biżuteria Na Zamówienie dla Elitarnych Gustów

In the lower right corner was the name:

Lukasiewicz Slep Jubilerski
Szeroka, 24
667 00 18

"That's a jewelry store, Rita," said Izolda. "In English it means, 'Custom Jewelry for Elite Tastes.' We need a camera."

Rita raced out of the basement, across the interior court-yard, through the tunnel to the front of the building, into the front door, up three flights of stairs and into her apartment. She left a minute later with her Polaroid camera, a plastic magnifying glass she had gotten in a box of cracker jacks and Motita Ruiz standing in the doorway hands on hips.

Through the magnifying glass they could read the street sign. One read *Szeroka* and the other *Miodowa*. The reflection of the lamp bulb and hot spots on the plastic made it impossible to take a picture and taking the photograph out of the sleeve was not an option. So Izolda picked up the lamp and put it on the cot mattress. Rita took three exposures at different distances, the last getting as close as she could before the image in her viewfinder went blurry. They both knew the old man would notice the slightest anomaly, so while the photographs dried, they pressed their dampened finger tips against the dried glue shards to lift them away and remove any indication the old man's space had been violated. As Izolda placed the envelope and scrap of paper back at the rear of the drawer, she took a ballpoint from her jean's pocket and wrote the three sets of two numbers on her palm.

They slowly backed out of the cubicle as they checked for traces they'd been there. There were none.

With Rita trailing, Izolda rushed to the circuit box saying, "I think these numbers are the combination to this lock. On the first attempt, forward, back and forward again the case and hasp separated. She opened the door. Both of them stood there gazing at neatly stacked quart cottage cheese containers that filled the entire three by five metal cabinet.

"There must be a hundred of them," gasped Izolda.

"He must be nuts," added Rita. "Let's get out of here."

Izolda quickly closed and locked the door, and they both took off giggling like children.

CHAPTER 18

There was hardly anyone on the boardwalk. Indian summer was hanging on for dear life. The beads of salted dew on the bench were now at the mercy of the rising sun and Moe's handkerchief. The unpainted lady sat down. Moe stood at the bench and watched a few joggers run by. A black care-giver lifted what was left of her charge out of her wheelchair, carried her down the stairs to the beach, trudged across the sand to a blanket, umbrella and beach chair already set up near the water's edge. The large black woman placed the frail white woman on the beach chair then rushed back to the boardwalk. As she collapsed the wheelchair and headed down the steps to the beach again, Moe shouted, "I'll probably be your next customer!"

"Not unless you lose a hundred pounds!" she shouted back.

"Then I better start dieting today."

"Don't waste your time, Moe. I'm retiring after this one. Save me six onion."

"They're at the register already, Gloria."

Moe continued to stand and scanned the pristine beach. He finally joined her and spoke.

"Look how new the beach looks. Yesterday this beach was covered with junk; cans, bottles, newspapers and food wrappers all over the place. The garbage baskets were over flowing with crap. And then an hour before sunset the garbage men made the beach new again."

He looked at her. "I sit here sometimes and think maybe I'll be as lucky as the beach. I'm littered with garbage. I'm overflowing with loneliness, self-pity and the memory of what Sylvia went through. So who knows? Maybe the garbage men will come one night and sweep all of it away and make me new again."

She turned toward him. "So that's what's happening here. You think I could be the garbage men."

"I don't know what I think," he answered. "Tell me your name."

She didn't respond.

"At least you owe me your name"

"Anna," she answered. "Now we're even."

CHAPTER 19

The Nor'easter found New York at noon. It slammed into the Hamptons, through the fragile bungalows of Rockaway, across the city and through the brick and mortar canyons of the North Bronx. It rained hard and then harder in the afternoon. The Indian summer was being swamped and a chill was replacing it. Izolda had rushed downstairs in her bathrobe just after sun up to caution the old man about going to work with the storm coming, but he wasn't there. She looked out of the window sporadically, called Berkowitz Furs. There was no answer. She figured they must have closed early or never opened and had no way to contact the old man about the closure.

By three o'clock she sat there, anxious, at the bedroom window imagining what might be happening to him.

The streets were empty except for the newspapers and other litter kidnapped by the wind and slammed into cars and buildings. She wondered if he was light enough to end up like the newspapers, but calmed herself knowing he had survived much worse and that sooner or later he'd appear from around the corner.

"Don't worry so much. I heard those people don't get wet," her husband laughed from the living room as he applied some silicone to the gaps in his botched air conditioner installation that rivulets of water were seeping through.

"Those people," she grimaced under her breath.

There was a knock at the door.

It was Rita. "He went to work in the middle of a storm?"

"The place is closed," responded Izolda.

"So where is he?"

"I think we should go downtown to his building the same way he does and see if he stopped somewhere."

"You want to go out in this mess?"

"He could be lying somewhere. We both know he won't ask for help."

"What if he's soaking wet on a train somewhere?"

"I'm going. You don't have to come."

CHAPTER 20

Cecilia was running out of pots and towels while Priscilla was buried under her comforter dreaming about floating on the azure waters off the beaches that ringed Mykonos, the last island her father had taken his spoiled princess to. She finally awoke when a branch hit the bedroom window. She looked out at the horizontal sheets of rain and the twigs and branches scattered everywhere. She threw on her bathrobe, went to the hallway and peered down over the balcony. She assumed Cecelia had waxed the Spanish-tiled floors glistening downstairs until she saw her exhausted 'maid' barefoot, slumped in the dining room doorway, the bottom of her night coat drenched.

"My God, are you okay?" Priscilla cried out.

"Welcome to the *Titanic*," Cecilia answered.

"Well, call someone to get it fixed."

"You have $37 in your checking account."

"Then take it from savings."

"Whose?"

CHAPTER 21

"Do all Jews eat so much?" murmured Anna as she swept the floors for the second time then mopped up the muddy shoe prints, spill residues, scuff marks and various unknowns.

"Bagels and lox are the Jew's sirens," said Moe. 'Most of my customers shouldn't go there, but they can't resist."

The strip mall was empty now. Diego had ended his work day. Anna sat down. Moe joined her.

"How's your beach today?" she asked.

"I'm okay. How are you?"

"I feel like a piece of wood."

"At least you're not floating on the Atlantic."

"What's the difference?"

"The difference is that you can have a fresh start."

"I don't think I started in the first place."

"What do you mean?"

"Nothing."

"Talk to me."

"About what?"

"About you."

"There is no me."

"About your accent, then. I have plenty of customers from south of the border. Where were you born?"

"Argentina."

"How did you end up here?"

"By bus."

"All the way from Argentina?"

"I hitched, took a bus when I could and had to screw for rides when I couldn't. That new career started somewhere between Matamoras and Corpus Christi. It took a year and hundreds of hot baths to get to Rockaway."

"Why Rockaway?" Moe asked.

"I felt out of place in Manhattan."

"What about family?"

"What family?"

"You have a mother and father?"

Anna got up, took off her apron. "I need time to think things out. I'm going to go back to my hotel."

"It's not a good idea, Anna."

"Do you have a better one?"

"I have a four-bedroom home, the last house at the beach at the end of the boardwalk on Fifteenth Street. The bus stop is a few minutes away. There's a beautiful view of the coast, the ocean and the Atlantic Beach Bridge. Two of the bedrooms have their own bathroom with a tub and shower."

"And you? Where will you be?" she asked.

"On the other side of the house in my own tub or shower."

"And what do you expect from me?"

"Twenty-five bucks a month rent, keep your room and bathroom nice, retire from your profession, do a good job behind the counter, and a conversation or two from time to time would be nice."

"Is that it?"

"Maybe we can go to dinner once a week."

"And is that all?"

"No. One of the bedrooms has its own twenty-inch color television and bathroom."

"You know what I mean," she persisted.

"Listen Anna, I don't know where or how you live, but believe me you shouldn't go back. You need a fresh start. Give life a chance. Are you close to here?"

"I don't know, Moe."

"No more streets for you. You have a job and me and Diego and a twenty-inch television."

She hesitated, leaned the mop against a table, then started walking toward the door.

Moe called out, "Where are you going?"

"To get my things, but I can't promise I won't disappoint you."

She hopped on a bus, and he followed. They got off a few blocks from the Palace.

"Stay here, she ordered. "I'll be back in ten minutes."

"You better be," he said.

Ten minutes later, he saw her walking toward him wearing a backpack and holding a legal-size manila envelope to her chest.

CHAPTER 22

They had double-checked the basement, walked to the subway checking out nooks and crannies on the way. Their subway car had been empty. Rita had checked all the cars forward and Izolda those to the rear even though they knew they knew the odds against his being on this particular train were humongous. They left the train and walked up to the street. The torrent was just a drizzle now. Streams of water swept refuse along the gutters against the curb and down into the sewers. Izolda took Rita's hand, they hopped over a raging rivulet and crossed the street to the corner coffee counter.

"How's my favorite Polish gumshoe this beautiful morning?" the man behind the counter asked Izolda.

"You didn't tell him someone was asking about him, did you?" she responded.

"You want some coffee, honey?"

"Did you?"

"Not a word. A promise is a promise."

"Did you see him today?"

"I told him Berkowitz was closed. He was drenched. I asked

him what the hell he was doing out in this mess. I asked him to come in out of the rain, but he took his egg sandwich and left. I yelled out that Berkowitz is closed, and I'll be closing up early. I'll take you home. He didn't even turn around."

Izolda and Rita high-tailed it down the street. He was sitting on a step against the brick wall of an entrance alcove. His eyes were closed. He was soaking wet and shivering. Half a drenched egg sandwich sat on its wrapper on his wet lap.

"Are you crazy?" yelled Izolda.

He opened his eyes. "Will you take me home?" he murmured.

"Why are you like this?" asked Rita.

"Take me home."

"Jesus Christ! Six million of your people died. Do you know how lucky you are?" pleaded Rita.

"If you're not going to take me home, leave me alone."

"Why don't you just walk in front of a goddamned bus," she screamed.

"I don't feel good," he whispered.

CHAPTER 23

"I've never been to Coney Island. I've never had a shrimp sandwich," said Anna, as she wiped the tartar sauce and ketchup from the sides of her mouth and chin.

"It was good, and so were the French fries."

"You're now the only Nathan's customer to leave without having a hot dog," chuckled Moe.

"Maybe next time," she said. "And I'll treat."

"Come," said Moe. "We'll sit on the boardwalk and watch the Gentiles on the Parachute Jump."

"Jews aren't allowed on the Parachute?" she asked.

"It's not that," answered Moe. "It's genetic."

"Tell me about them," she asked."

"Tell you about who?"

"Jews."

"What do you want to know about us?"

"Everything."

"I'll make you a deal. You ask me a question, and I'll ask you a question. Are you in?"

She shrugged and nodded.

"You can go first," said Moe.

"Why do Jews cause so much trouble?"

"What kind of trouble?"

"You know, all kinds of trouble."

"Can't you be more specific?"

Anna shrugged again.

"Have you ever had trouble with Jews?" asked Moe.

"I've had plenty of Jewish customers, but I never really knew any until I met you."

"So, how am I doing?"

"I heard such bad things about Jews while I was growing up."

"Did you?" reacted Moe. "There are four billion people on the planet and only 13 million Jews. How much trouble can we make? You have to be more specific, Anna."

"No I don't, Moe. Our game is over. Let's go back."

"Anna, who said those 'bad things?'"

"If you don't want to go back, I can take the bus."

"Just one more question. You told me, but I forgot. Where were you born?"

"Bariloche, Argentina. Are or are you not taking me back to my room?"

CHAPTER 24

Motita Ruiz had no competition when it came to her sopa di pollo. The sweet, oniony aroma flooded the apartment, the corridors and took the elevator to the lobby where it was as inviting as a welcome mat.

Threats of calling for an ambulance had cajoled the old man into accepting the attention of the lady and the girl who were sitting on the two folding chairs facing him one on each side of his cot. He sat in bed, his back against the wall, pillow on his lap finishing yet another bowl of the magic potion. That day was the first in which he was able to get the spoon to his mouth without Izolda or Rita holding his shaking hand. The towel-bib on his chest and lap didn't have to visit a washing machine for the first time in four days. He had been prone for most of the time loaded with fever and Anacin. Izolda had changed his soaking wet sheet and pillow case several times while the fever broke. He had seen the worry in Rita's eyes as she put cold compresses on his forehead. Now he was out of danger. Now he was wasn't shaking. Now he had been needy and accepted help for the first time in decades.

"You looked better when you had fever," said Rita. "Your face had some color in it."

The old man reached out, took her hand and clenched it. His faded blue eyes scanned her face as if discovering it for the first time. He managed, "How old are you?"

"Fourteen," she answered.

He closed his eyes and was off somewhere.

CHAPTER 25

The Hamptons had been through the rains and wind and come out the other side as fresh and serene as ever. The odd couple, facing the house, sat next to each other on chaises disappearing in the overgrown lawn. They watched as the last edge of the blue tarp was affixed to the roof that would cost twenty thousand to replace if, in fact, Priscilla could raise the money. When the workmen were finished, the ladies went inside, dressed up in their 'we really don't need the money' outfits and headed for the bank.

The condition of the Cates Southampton mansion was proof that Cecilia Papouloute had been hired for the wrong job. She was no housemaid. She had graduated from the University of Haiti with a business and management degree and, after five years of participating in every facet of the family's quadrille manufacturing business in Port-au-Prince, was running the business while her activist mother, father and sister concentrated on clandestine activities to depose the devil that governed their country.

While her parents and sister were sleeping or plotting, she taught herself to take apart and put together every machine and piece of equipment in the place and learned enough about motors, electrical and plumbing to keep strangers out of the shop.

***

On an otherwise perfect afternoon, Cecilia was returning from collecting woven piece goods from the artisans scattered about the island when an employee carrying a wicker suitcase jumped in front of her car a block away from the factory and beckoned her into an alley. Through her sobs, the seamstress described the scene of Cecilia's mother, father and sister being taken away by armed men and that those men were waiting for her at the factory and her home.

"Run, Boss, run! You know you'll never see them again. Run as fast as you can away from this purgatory."

Cecilia Papouloute had no time to cry or mourn. She knew that her family would disappear into the manufactured hell of Papa Doc Duvalier for speaking out opposition against his regime.

The wicker suitcase was filled with layered cut piece goods to make the blouses and matching skirts that created the Quadrille or Karabella as she called them and all the cash the workers could grab from the till, desk drawers and what they could barely afford from their pockets and handbags.

Cecilia parked in the alley until nightfall and then drove across Haiti to Port de Pais and the rickety boat that made the horrific journey to the Bahamas and Florida. After a few days of sleeping and mourning in a vacant warehouse in Key West she borrowed a magic marker from one of the vendors at an outdoor Farmer's Market, took apart a large cardboard box and serpentine'd her way in and around the aisles with a sign that read:

'I WILL COOK THE BEST WEST INDIAN FOOD AND KEEP YOUR BOAT TIDY FOR FOUR HUNDRED DOLLARS AND A LIFT TO NEW YORK. I WILL TELL YOU WHAT SPICES TO BUY.

As the vendors packed up, a boat repair-poor-couple who were buying provisions before sailing back to New York, didn't have the four-hundred dollars but, agreed to drop her off at Greenpoint, Long Island, the town her aunt and uncle had fled to the year before. What Cecilia didn't know was that they didn't make it. By the time her journey was over, so was her ability to keep food down for a few days. She saw a help wanted sign in a dry cleaning store's window in Southampton and was hired on the spot becoming the most over-qualified shirt presser in dry cleaning history. Pricilla Cates thought she had proselytized a hard-working skeleton that did housework and ended up with an eating machine that was proficient at all things except housecleaning.

***

Mr. Peterson, vice president, chief guardian, protector of the hundreds of millions at the Hamptons Saving and Loan, sat at his desk looking at the couple sitting opposite him: an early-forties fidgety white woman and a thin pitch-black woman in some sort of colorful garb who stared right through him.

"Ms. Cates, you've never had a job or taken out a loan and paid it back."

"What about the home equity loan?"

"Your father arranged that, and there's still a sizable balance and the matter of unpaid property taxes."

"Who do you think's been paying it back?"

"You inherited the loan and back taxes. We know you've been making the payments, and we've been working with you, but it's his loans. You have no track record."

He turned to Cecilia and chuckled, "If she had Wilma Rudolph's track record she'd be walking out of here with the money in a New York minute."

Cecilia Papouloute squinted and craned forward, "How did you guess I was black?"

"I'm sorry, ma'am. I'm a big fan."

Cecilia's engine kept running. "In other words, if Miss Cates was black and fast there'd be no problem?"

"I'm sorry. I never inten–"

"Well, I'm black and fast. I medaled in track and field at The University of Haiti while I was working on my MBA. I'll take out the loan."

"I'm sorry."

"About what?" she shot back.

"I truly didn't mean it that way."

"What way?"

"It was just a play on words."

"Play with these words: What about our house as collateral?"

"I'm sorry. There's still a balance, and this bank is not in the real estate business…and then there's her father."

Priscilla's back stiffened. "What about my father?"

"Alas, getting paid back by your father was like getting blood from a stone, and even if our history with him was perfect, memories are not collateral, Ms. Cates."

Cecilia jumped in. "Alas, my ass! Since when do the sins of the father have anything to do with a daughter?"

"Does the apple fall far from the tree?" he countered.

"What if the tree is on a hill?" She shot back.

He leaned across his desk toward Priscilla as he addressed her.

"Don't let this one out of your sight." He extended his card toward Cecilia. "If she does let you out of her sight, come to see me before you accept another position."

They left the bank and headed home. The phone message awaiting Priscilla Cates displaced her concerns about the roof and her maid. It was from a whispering Mrs. Greenfeld in apartment 4c.

"I thought you should know, Miss Cates, that Mr. Nowicki was offered a job by the owner of the new building down the block."

CHAPTER 26

It's as if a reset button was pressed after the wind and rain cleansed and polished the neighborhood. There's something about the sky, the streets, the grass, the shiny leaves, the glistening windows of the apartment buildings and storefronts that seemed to say, "Let's start over again."

There was something about the old man that made it impossible for him to start over again. There was no reset button. There was no future, only the past.

The girls cajoled him into leaving the cube and going to the park for a few hours. They left him sitting there while they returned and prepared a "surprise." Soon he would be back to work weak or not. His gait was slower and his joints ached. He sat on the park bench looking at his knuckles scarred from thousands of encounters with the sharp tips of staples while he was combing them out of the fur skins stretching on plywood four by eights leaning against the shop walls. He looked at the tattoos on his forearm and closed his eyes. He opened them a few minutes later, then sat there continuing to contemplate what letting these two women into his life might mean for the rest of it. He sat there nervous, pondering if the life he had deserved was being threatened.

Rita returned a few hours later, took him by the arm and walked him back to the building. Izolda was standing in the cube's doorway grinning. Rita let go of his arm. Izolda bowed and gestured he take a look inside. He walked to the doorway and looked in. The small wardrobe opposite the door was the first thing he saw. The door was open. His few things were hanging on hangers inside. An old standing lamp with an imitation Tiffany shade dispersed colored shards of light on the wall and ceiling, and a small standing shelf unit with a framed map of Poland above it was against the wall to his left. An old rocking chair waited for its new occupant next to a shelf with an ancient Bakelite radio sitting on it playing classical music, its power cord traveling down to an extension cord to the only outlet in the cube. Another cord with a gang plug at its end hugged the wall, went over the door stapled beneath the transom and down the wall to a gang plug and a space heater.

The centerpiece of the surprise was a box spring and mattress with a fresh new pillow, white sheet and duvet. A small embroidered pillow read, *Don't Worry Be Happy.*

They guided him to the chair, sat him down. He hung on to the arms as they rocked him gently a few times. Both took off his sneakers and socks, walked him to the edge of the bed, lifted his legs and gently rotated them onto the mattress. Rita took the embroidered pillow away and Izolda eased him down onto the bed and plush pillow. He lay there saying nothing looking up at the ceiling.

"Well, how's it feel?" asked Rita.

He continued to stare at the ceiling. The ladies waited a minute or so, looked at each other, then left him. Rita returned to her proud mom and dad. She thanked her father for helping with the bed. Izolda returned to her livid husband who was ready and waiting to make her pay one way or another for disregarding his order to leave well enough alone and respect his wishes.

A week later, Rita and Izolda found a package at their door wrapped in newspaper and tied with bakery string. Inside each was a pair of mink mittens.

CHAPTER 27

Anna, prone on a beach blanket, was asleep on her stomach facing the boardwalk a few yards from the undulating line of foam the receding ripples left behind. Diego sat facing the sea, arms wrapped around his knees hunching forward. It was just after Labor Day. They were the only people on the beach. He turned to see if she was sleeping and saw the turquoise cameo pendant resting on the blanket a few inches from the back of her neck. He lied down on his side and, leaving some slack in the chain, gently picked up the pendant and studied it. The front was a carved image of a beautiful woman's face. The setting was a narrow gold frame with four prongs hugging the cameo to it. There was a trace of worn script etched into the unfinished back of the cameo. He couldn't read what it said. He faced it toward the sun at various angles, but it was still illegible. She sat up. The pendant jerked out of his hands.

"And what are you up to?" she asked.

"I was trying to read what it said."

"Why?"

"I don't know. What does it say?"

"I have no idea. It's too worn out. It's been that way since I had it."

"A jeweler could use that thing they put in their eye or maybe there's something they could put on it to make the writing come out. Wouldn't you like to know what it says?"

She shrugged.

"Where did you get it?"

"I found it."

"Where?"

"Enough! Let's get back to the store."

"Why don't you ever talk about your past?"

"My past disappeared. One day I had one. The next day it was gone."

"What about your parents?"

"The same. One day I had them. The next day they were gone."

"What happened?"

"They both died. They were driving to Patagonia and drove into a tree."

"How old were you?"

"I was eleven."

"Christ, Anna, I'm sorry."

"It was for the best," she answered indifferently.

Diego didn't believe what he heard. "For the best?"

"Yes, it was for the best. They were both very sick people."

"Do you think they did it on purpose?"

"Yes."

"I can think of better ways to end it all," Diego continued.

"I guess they couldn't," she shot back.

"Where did you go? What happened to you?"

"That's it. I'm heading back to the store."

She sprung up and headed toward the boardwalk. He grabbed the beach blanket and caught up to her.

Halfway up the boardwalk steps, Diego grabbed the back of her shirt. She turned, looked down at him.

"Anna, you act like a mouse and everyone else is a cat."

He let go of her shirt tail and continued talking as they walked across the boardwalk to the street side.

Diego continued, "After my dad died, Moe stepped in like a father. Now he's doing the same for you. Have you ever had a real friend, someone you can talk to?"

She continued up the stairs then turned around.

"It was my mother's," said the unpainted lady.

CHAPTER 28

Soon, autumn would be bullied out of the way by winter. The trees in the park would go bald. The tenacious few remaining brown leaves that had hung on to the branches of the oaks and elms for dear life would succumb to the wind, the weight of snow and sleet. Frost would make the park sparkle. The benches would glow, and on the streets and roads surrounding the park, on too many nights and early mornings, black ice would render brakes useless.

The ancient Bakelite radio sat on the shelf creating its magic. Classical music played day and night; a comforting murmur that made the cube a home. The old man no longer went to the park. On this Sunday he caught himself humming along with Brahms first symphony, then turned the radio off after he had laced his sneakers.

Sunday was always a day off, but he had agreed to come in on this one after Berkowitz had sent his son to ask him when he would be back and added that his pop was way behind on orders and a nervous wreck. No one could remove staples with a staple comb as fast as the old man could without leaving marred pelts in its wake. Today the magician would eliminate the roadblock so the cutters could cut, sewers could sew and finishers could create the coats that would thrill wives, girlfriends and mistresses. Almost all his coworkers would be there. He wasn't the only one that had been home with the flu.

Later that morning, Izolda and Rita were sitting on the building's front steps when the carriage passed by. The mom walked along side, her hand adjusting the blanket swaddling her treasure. The grandparents, one holding each side of the carriage handle, pushed the carriage and the gift their son and daughter had given them without taking their eyes off that gift. Izolda looked at the procession and closed her eyes searching images and then opened them.

"Rita, we have work to do."

"What kind of work?" asked Rita.

CHAPTER 29

The driving instructor asked Cecilia if the car they were in was hers. "No it's my boss's," she answered.

"Well I guess it's better to learn on a stick because you kill two birds with one stone," he added.

"I don't have a stone, and even if I did, I don't kill birds."

"You know what I mean, ma'am. You'll be able to drive an automatic also."

"Brilliant," murmured his student shaking her head.

"She pulled up to the house, ran inside, ran back, handed him a check. He signed copies of the driver's education completion form and handed her the copy.

"I'll submit this tomorrow. You'll get your permanent license in a week or two. You did very well. A bit too aggressive a few times, but it's obvious you've driven before."

"For thousands of miles up and down hills, mountains and through city traffic. I've driven along the edge of a four thousand foot drop on a dirt road as wide as my car."

As he headed for his, he said, "There's no 4000-foot drop around here, just thousands of lousy drivers, Use your mirrors, and don't drive at night until your permanent license comes."

She nodded an okay knowing she'd probably be returning from the Bronx after dark, but that would only be a problem if she screwed up and she never did.

Priscilla Cates left the den window and started to dress. In fifteen minutes she would be chauffeured by her housemaid to the Bronx, the other side of the world, to her only source of income and Mr. Nowicki, the gatekeeper.

CHAPTER 30

The Jade Garden provided the last meal of the week for Moe and the majority of Jewish Chinese food lovers in the Rockaways and its environs. Anna had picked up Chinese food during her year-long odyssey from Mendoza to Rockaway, but she had never dined in a Chinese restaurant. Crowds made her nervous, but for the first time in memory she was calm, not self-conscious and felt she was one of them and not an anomaly living on the periphery of humankind. She reached across the table and took Moe's hands.

"Look, I might not be the garbage men cleaning your beach, but I'm happy to be here for you like you've been for me." She tightened her grip. Tears started to flow down her cheeks. She tilted her head down and started to sob quietly.

Moe lifted her napkin and put it in her hands that were hugging her face. "This is good. Let it out, and then we'll talk."

They didn't.

CHAPTER 31

While Priscilla and Cecelia were on the way to Nowicki, the old man was on his way to work. He felt chilled, but the air wasn't cold. The subway seats seemed harder, but they were the same as always. He found it more challenging to remain upright during the squealing curves and not lean into the half-asleep book ends on either side of him. Since he recovered, his body felt older. He remembered reading that at seventy; it takes a week to regain the strength lost after one day in bed. He couldn't care less. 'Just do a day at a time,' he said to himself. 'Do a day at a time until it's over, until purgatory becomes hell.'

The stairs from the bowels of Manhattan to the street seemed endless. He had to stop at each landing. It took him longer to cross Seventh Avenue and get to his egg sandwich and decaf.

"How are you feeling?" asked the owner.

"I'm okay," he answered.

"You're a lucky man."

"That's how I got my name," he said.

"You're lucky and fortunate. I never hear from my family. Yours came out in a hurricane to find you."

"How do you know that?" the old man asked.

"Your granddaughters were frantic looking for you."

"They're not my granddaughters."

"Then you should adopt them. They were really worried about you."

The old man put down a crumpled dollar bill and some change and headed to the building. His coat found the same hook it spent the day on for twenty-five years, but not his vest. He never took his vest off. Berkowitz, sitting in his office on the other side of an interior window he could see the entire shop through, smiled and nodded his hello. The few employees on the floor didn't seem happy about having to work on a Sunday. The old man grabbed a step stool and headed for the first dried pelt stapled to a plywood four by eight leaning against the wall. Berkowitz couldn't take his eyes off him throughout the day. The old man used to reach the top of the skin while standing on the floor. Now he needed the step stool. Gravity had stolen almost two inches from him since he was hired. Berkowitz watched as he fought to keep his balance on the way up and waivered when he reached the top. He combed the staples at the top of the pelt then descended one step at a time to work the middle and bottom.

On a few occasions, when the old man wavered, Berkowitz jumped off his high stool and started toward him, but the old man regained his balance and refused help.

His fate was decided while he was on his fifth pelt, a sable that would be ready in a week or so for its old money Park Avenue owner and her fiftieth anniversary.

As soon as he grabbed his coat at closing time, Berkowitz called him into his office.

"In the forty years I've been in business, I've never had an employee like you. You've done everything you've been asked to do. You've never asked for anything. I've had to convince you to take every raise. Believe me you deserved more than you were being paid."

"What are you telling me, Mr. Berkowitz?"

"Aaron, do you go to the movies?"

The old man shook his head, no.

"There's a movie called *The Invisible Man*. You've made yourself invisible until now. For twenty-five years you walked in the door, did your job and left. You talked to no one and did what you were asked to do, but you were invisible. Dear Aaron, I should have taken a movie of you on that step stool the last few months. You almost lost your balance on every step. You're no longer invisible. I won't let you get on one again."

"Please, Mr. Berkowitz, I don't want you to let me go."

"You almost died from pneumonia. My wife is not well. Our kids and grandkids live all over the place. We don't see them enough, so we're going to start visiting them. I'm like you. When I work I give it everything. Now I find myself sitting on that fucking stool too much. I'm selling the business, and you don't want to work for the young turk and his father who's buying it. And even if you did, you wouldn't have the arrangement that we have so you can also collect social security."

He handed an envelope to the old man.

"Aaron, don't open the envelope until you get home. Inside is my card with my home number if you want to keep in touch and a little something to help with your retirement."

"You called me Aaron, Mr. Berkowitz. It's the first time anyone anywhere has called me by my first name since Europe. It was nice to hear my name."

"Mine is Simon. Aaron…Aaron, you are a miracle. Twenty-five years and not one damaged pelt. Only God knows how much money you saved me. You are a true artist and a good human being, but it has always seemed that you didn't think you were either. Aaron, if you ever decide you want the company of other people, please extend my wife, Susan, and I the first invitation."

"Thank you, Simon. Thanks for the job. Thank you for the twenty-five years."

"God bless you and stay healthy, Aaron."

"God took a look at me years ago and crossed me off his blessing list. Good bye, Simon. Say goodbye to everyone for me. I hope your wife gets better and you see more of your children."

Simon Berkowitz extended his hand. The old man took it. They looked at each other for a moment, then let go. Both men knew they were saying goodbye to a life's work and faced the specter of being useless.

The old man put on his coat over his vest and walked across the shop to the stairs. He looked down the steep flight to the street and a life he was unfamiliar with. When he reached the bottom stair, he sat on it and was lost in thought until he remembered the envelope. There were fifty crisp one hundred dollar bills, a paycheck and a note.

"Like it or not you're alive, and you're a good man. I don't know what troubles you, but it's time to treat yourself to a little happiness. Believe me Aaron; it's more important than the money."

CHAPTER 32

Moe was still in the shop when Diego and Anna returned from the beach. He stopped them at the door. "Turn around and wipe that sand off your feet. I just finished mopping the floors."

Diego looked around. "Good job, boss. I think we'll go back to the beach and frolic while you do the display cases."

"I needed the exercise and so do you. Do the display cases before school tonight and you can have the morning off."

"And you, my Anna, my favorite female frolicker, please get the water spots off the glasses tonight, and you can also have the morning off. Make them sparkle like you."

They wiped the sand off their feet and walked in. Moe stowed the mop and pail, grabbed his coat and took off.

When they were done, Diego made them both a cup of coffee and they sat at a table.

"I'm going to the 42nd Street Library tomorrow to check out some stuff for my Latin American history term paper. Have you been on The Long Island Railroad?"

"I've only been downtown a couple of weeks when I first came here," answered Anna.

"Have you been to the library?"

"No."

"Then come with me. I'll only need an hour or so, and you can check out all they have on mystery women."

"I'm no mystery, Diego. I worked the streets, and now I don't. Do they have a retired hooker section?"

"You weren't a hooker."

"I wasn't?"

"You weren't a hooker when you were a hooker. I think you were only a temp. C'mon, come downtown with me."

"Diego, promise me you won't pry anymore."

"No hay problema. Moe said you'll let us in when you're ready. And if you're never ready that's okay too."

CHAPTER 33

The car hadn't budged from the driveway. Priscilla had chosen the back seat to be further away from the collision not Cecilia.

"There are three vacancies in the building," thought Priscilla out loud. "My father must be chewing on the velvet. What if Mrs. Greenfeld was right? What if I make Nowicki mad? What if he goes to the other building?"

"What if? What if? What if?!" Cecelia shot back.

"Lady, he won't bite, and for God's sake, give yourself some credit! Your father must have donated one of his genes to you. Come sit up front. I don't want to be a chauffeur today."

Priscilla joined her and off they went.

Murray Cates's daughter had not been on a highway since she was taken to the ophthalmologist in Manhattan when she was twelve. Her eyesight was fine now even though she couldn't see beyond the Hamptons and Fire Island. The car left the rural climes of Suffolk County and entered the alien Nassau and Queens County and then went onto the Cross Bronx Expressway morphing into one section of a mechanical caterpillar inching its way through a jungle of worn apartment buildings and concrete.

By the time they had left the expressway and were nearing Riverdale, her father's genes had made their debut, and Priscilla suspected she had been in hiding and dependent on others for no good reason. She opened the passenger window and breathed in the alien aromas of the real world and her confidence grew. As they pulled up in front of her building, not her father's, they stopped a few feet from Nowicki sitting on the curb smoking a cigarette. He rose and walked over to the driver's window. He motioned to Cecilia to lower it. He looked down at her. The embroidered *SUPERINTENDENT* on his breast pocket was a foot from her face.

"The building's fully rented," he said, smiling. "Try the buildings further south from here. There are plenty of vacancies for you down there."

Cecilia pointed at the vacancy sign.

"Oh, I forgot to take that down. Take care, ladies."

He turned to leave.

Priscilla's eyes narrowed to slits and her jaws clenched. She rolled down her window and called out, "I'm Priscilla Cates. Why do we have three vacancies?"

He returned to the window.

"So you finally came to see our building."

"No," answered Priscilla still fueled by the no vacancy bullshit. "I didn't come to see *our* building. I thought it was about time we met."

"Then meet we will. Come to my apartment. I'll make some tea and we have cookies my wife baked."

The ladies left the car and followed Nowicki up the front steps, into the building and into his apartment a few feet from the front door. Izolda was off somewhere. Nowicki led them to the kitchen table and put up some water.

"In Poland, there's always hot water waiting for tea and a wife who's there to serve it. My wife is an American now. I don't know where she is half the time."

"Is that a bad thing?" Priscilla asked.

"Your father was a tough man," reacted Nowicki. "Are you like him?"

"No one was like my father."

"We have no children, so I treat this building like it's my daughter. I know that your father liked that. But maybe you think that's a problem?"

"You tell me, Mr. Nowicki."

"The old man is a Jew just like you, and he keeps to himself."

"Just like me?" asked Priscilla.

"Miss Cates, I decided that if I took the few dollars I would never have to bother your father for a raise or a bonus."

"Was it a tough decision for you?" Cecelia asked.

Priscilla hushed her with eyes.

"And what about the washers and dryers?" asked Priscilla. "I haven't seen a nickel from them."

"I admit I use the change to fix things around the building and also pay the people who fix things for me. Your father knew what I was doing and didn't care."

"He never said a word about it to me. Why don't you let me decide who and what gets paid with what."

"Miss Cates, your father would have wanted that I save you the problems."

"How thoughtful of you and my father, Mr. Nowicki. Let me ask you another question."

"Go girl," Cecelia whispered under her breath.

"What about the liability and fire insurance? Who do you think would be sued if something happened to the building and the tenants because of him? A claim could ruin me."

"Miss Cates, he's like a feather. He comes and goes like a ghost. He bothers no one."

"Mr. Nowicki, why are there three apartments vacant for the first time?" asked Priscilla.

"That's not my fault," he shot back. "There's a beautiful new building a block from here and they have central air and a meeting room tenants can have parties in."

"Have you been trying to rent the apartments?"

"Of course. I never had to list vacancies before. And now, more problems. Another new building is going up right on the park, and I think some people are waiting to see what it looks like and the rents they want. Also, there's some Puerto Ricans my wife leased into our building without asking me. That doesn't help."

"Do they have cholera?" asked Cecelia, head tilted.

"Mr. Nowicki is there anything else you want to tell me?" asked Priscilla.

"Miss Cates, if you're unhappy with me I want to know."

"Why would I be unhappy with you?" she continued. "You were only trying to protect me."

"What about the old man's rent?" he asked.

"I want to see his apartment."

"He's not in an apartment. That's the whole thing. He's in a room I nailed together in the basement. He isn't comfortable with people."

"I'm not 'people.' I'm his landlord. I want to talk to him."

"He's at work."

Please take me to his 'room.'"

"Follow me… It's not exactly a room."

They went through the passageway to the rear of the building and into the basement. Priscilla stood in front of the three unfinished drywalls that were bolted to each other and the exterior cinderblock wall. Nowicki opened his door, and the ladies looked in.

"Where's his bathroom?" asked Priscilla.

Nowicki pointed to the jury-rigged set up across the basement.

"Do you know what building codes are, Mr. Nowicki?"

"Of course, but inspectors have their hands full in the South Bronx. They never bother me."

"Does it bother you that another human being lives like this?"

"It was his idea. He was living in the park. He doesn't like to be with people."

"Things have to change, Mr. Nowicki." said Priscilla.

"Miss Cates, I've given everything to this building and your father and you. If you're unhappy with me just tell me."

"For now, put an ad in the paper, and ask the old man if he can pay what it costs to live like a human."

"And if he can't?"

"This isn't a shelter."

"You're the boss. Whatever you say."

As they left the basement, they didn't notice Izolda and Rita outside, backs pressed against brick to the left of the door to the yard. They had been listening to the entire conversation.

CHAPTER 34

The dazed old man had passed his subway entrance and kept walking uptown. He walked north one or two streets at a time before walking east and up the next avenue. For years, Manhattan could have been abandoned, and he wouldn't have noticed. Now, for some reason, he took it all in. With no agenda or destination, he found himself observing details. He looked up at the movie theater marquees, at people pouring into the street after late mass. He looked at the throng of people promenading on both sides of Fifth Avenue, at displays in store windows, at the gigantic signs on and above buildings. He passed under the Winston man blowing smoke rings over his head. He was gliding through a parallel world he hadn't visited since he ended up in New York.

He was on Forty-Fourth Street passing Papaya King. A woman wrapped in rags sat on the sidewalk, her back against brick and the store window, legs splayed over concrete, bare feet the color of cement. She sat staring forward asking for nothing, He thought about the park and how many nights he sat against the elm. The old man took the envelope from his pocket, took out a hundred dollar bill, bent over and handed it to her. She looked at it.

"Do you want me to change it to smaller amounts for you?" he asked.

"No, that's not necessary. They'll give you change when you buy me the hot dog," she answered matter-of-factly.

He started to open the door when she added, "Mustard and ketchup, sautéed onions not sauerkraut, and tell them it's for Mrs. Preston and they'll give you extra fries and a Coke, and get something for yourself. You don't look so good."

He left her holding the hot dog and fries and continued to walk up town and across to Avenue of the Americas. It was a few minutes to four when he passed a line of people hugging a building to his right and turning onto Fifty-Seventh Street. He followed them, and in a few steps was in front of Carnegie Hall. The name, Adam Harasiewicz, was everywhere. And so were the *Sold Out* signs taped over everything. The pianist was Polish and so was, Chopin, whose works he was performing. He stood there until the crowd thinned. Now there were only a few forlorn people mulling about looking for ticket scalpers willing to sell their souls for a seat. He was about to turn away and leave when a couple dashed out of the door. The man called out for a taxi. The woman extended two tickets toward the old man.

"We've had an emergency. He's a great pianist." He looked at her, at the tickets. A cab pulled up. She shoved them toward him. He took them. They jumped into the cab and off they went. The last call chime sounded in the street. Oblivious to the offers for his extra ticket, he entered the recital hall, was given a program and was escorted to fourth row center.

The couple next to him asked if the empty seat was taken. He nodded no. They put their coats and her bag on it and thanked him. The pianist entered from the wings. The audience rose and applauded. It was more movement and sound the old man had been engulfed in since his wedding. He glanced down at the program. The first piece was Chopin's Mazurka Opus 17 Number 4. His mind raced back and returned. He hoped he could make it through the fourteen minutes. The pianist caressed the first phrase. Tears started flowing after a few bars, sobs soon after. He rose, oblivious to the impact his departure created, moved up the aisle and rushed outside onto Fifty-Seventh Street. He felt he had to get back to his room while he could still function, before memories catapulted him back to the emptiness. As he approached the subway entrance, he slowed down, hesitated and then forced himself to walk into Central Park instead. He sat and watched the boys and girls playing, the boaters peddling. A peregrine falcon sat on a bare branch on top of a London Plane tree looking for a convenient snack. He thought about the pianist and the girl and woman who cared about him. He thought about Mr. Simon Berkowitz and his kindness. He thought about Chopin's nocturne and that it survived the death of Poland and now lived in the present and would live on in the future. And, for the first time in memory, he caught himself thinking about the rest of his life and not the end of it. But those thoughts soon evaporated on the way home.

CHAPTER 35

Anna chose to sit on the library steps beneath one of the massive concrete lions while Diego was inside gleaning what he needed from the several books on his table. He had invited her to go in with him and enjoy the architecture, but she chose the cool air and the space to the library. He cautioned her about Times Square and assured her that he wouldn't be more than an hour or so. She knew about 42nd Street and the reputation. She sat for a bit, rose, walked uptown to the corner and made a left, east toward the decadence to see for herself. The devil's oasis sitting in the center of Manhattan Island on 42nd Street between Seventh and Eighth was a home for the dark side and seemed like the first stop on a journey to hell. Anna walked up and down passed visitors, hookers, freaks, porn stores, theaters and various temptations for those from other places whose fantasies were impossible to act upon in the podunks of the world. She had not worn makeup since Moe rescued her from herself. Now her hair was in a ponytail, and she wore Birkenstock sandals not heels. Most of the time she felt like a new person, but for a few fleeting moments she felt the tether, the tug to her past. She looked at the hookers beckoning boys and men and women and girls old and young with their glances and more. She looked at the caked makeup, false lashes and eye shadow but felt like an observer. Perhaps Diego was right, she thought to herself. She wasn't one of them. She was never one of them. She probably was just visiting the profession, sweating out the past, on the way to finding her place in the world. She felt the remains of the tether come undone, and she was elated. On the way back to the library she stopped at a cosmetic store. She bought a lipstick and some blush. She left the store looking and feeling like she was ready to take on the rest of her life.

Diego packed up his pads and pencils. As he left, he passed by Izolda Nowicki and Rita Ruiz reading and taking notes from separate copies of *Polish Jews and the Holocaust*.

He walked out squinting through the bright sunlight. Diego didn't recognize Anna at first. It wasn't the sun or the makeup, it was her demeanor. She grabbed him under the arm and cajoled him to walk uptown toward Central Park.

When they approached 47th Street, he suggested they grab a bite at the pizza place on the corner. She ate two slices, shared a calzone and powdered her lips with a cannoli. They left the place and continued across town. There were jewelry stores and diamond exchanges lining both sides of the street. A few doors down from the pizza place, a man wearing a yarmulke, bent over like a question mark, sat inside a shop window looking through a loop at something in a mini-vise.

"He's what I meant," exclaimed Diego pointing at him. "He'll be able to read the scribbling."

"Why is it so important to you?" she asked.

"You're important to me," he answered.

He tapped on the glass. The man looked up and buzzed them in. "I'll be with you in a few minutes. There are some pieces in the jewelry case if you've saved up enough money."

He returned to the loop.

They stood there until he looked up.

"What can I do for you?"

Diego removed the cameo pendant from Anna's neck. "We're hoping you could read what it says on the back."

"And then what?" the man asked.

"We'll say thank you and walk to Central Park"

"What a deal! Thank God you came along. Business was lousy today. Give it to me." He examined the front and back through the loop and shook his head. "This could be a tough one," he cautioned as he sat down. He looked up at Anna. "Where did you get this?"

"I didn't. It was my mother's," she answered.

"I usually can tell where someone is from by their accent, but yours is difficult. Where are you from?"

"Argentina."

"I have a beautiful customer from Argentina, and you sound different."

"Argentina's a big country," reacted Anna.

He returned to the cameo. "You know most people rub stain or something on the back to make the writing come out. Sometimes they use tea or coffee or lemon juice, but they don't know that soft turquoise like this stains too easily."

"Thanks anyhow," said Anna, as she reached over the counter for the piece. He raised his palm to stop her.

"I said most people, but I'm not most people. Keep an eye on the piece of glass in the vise, and I'll be right back."

He left and returned carrying a tin.

"This is talcum powder," he said. "If I put some on the back and blow it off, some stays in the engraving even though it's almost gone. Then I rub it with my finger and the oil plus a bit of schmutz stain the talcum powder and later a little soap and water and it's gone. Watch."

He sprinkled on some powder, blew it away and gently rubbed the back.

"This looks like it was sanded," the jeweler murmured to himself."

Transfixed on what he saw through the loop, he turned and looked at them quizzically.

"Are either of you Jewish?" he asked.

I'm Catholic, and she's, he turned to Anna. "What are you?"

"I'm Catholic," she whispered.

"Then where did you get this?" he asked suspiciously.

"It was stuck in the tread of some tires I stole." Diego answered, his hand extended. "I'll take it, and we'll let you get back to the piece of glass."

"Wait a minute. Wait a minute. I apologize if I was impolite." He put the cameo on the counter. "Come, take the loop and see why I'm surprised." He beckoned them closer.

Diego looked first. "It looks like scribbling."

"What else do you see?"

Diego took another look. "I just see scribbling."

"Do you know if someone sanded this?" asked the jeweler.

"Why would anyone do that?" reacted Diego.

The jeweler looked toward Anna. "Come, look uh. I'm sorry I don't know your name."

"Her name is Anna," Diego answered for her.

"Anna, a nice Spanish name," said the jeweler. "Come take a look."

"Let's leave," she insisted.

"Please excuse me. This is a mystery to me," said the jeweler.

"Why?" asked Diego.

"It's Yiddish. The writing is Yiddish. Anna, do you know how your mother got this?"

"No."

"You have no idea?" the jeweler persisted.

"No."

"Are you sure your parents didn't have Jews in the family?"

"We have to go," Anna insisted. "Let's go, Diego."

Diego didn't budge.

"Dear, where was she from, your mother?"

"Argentina."

"She was born there?"

"She was born and died in Argentina. Why are you asking all these questions of us?" asked Anna.

"No reason, dear. It's my nature. Would you like to know what it says?"

Diego and Anna stood there.

He read the inscription:

טייר ןיימ וצ

ץראה עצנאג ןיימ טסיב וד

"It says, *To my Ruth, You are my whole heart.* And along the bottom is the name of the artist the date and number of the piece: *g.cotto 27.6.1937 nu: 31783.*"

"All that?" said Diego.

"Do either of you like classical music?" asked the jeweler.

They just stood there.

"*Dein bist meine ganzes hertz* is a song from a Franz Lehar operetta. 'You are my whole heart,' really means 'you are my whole life.' The man who gave the woman this piece really loved the woman he gave it to. Hitler, the two-faced sadistic pig, made Lehar's Jewish wife, Sophie, an honorary Aryan, so his favorite composer would continue writing. Every other Jew connected to him including most of the musicians that recorded his favorite operettas ended up ashes in Dachau. They say in his final month, the pig listened only to *The Merry Widow*, which Lehar also wrote. The Victrola in the bunker had the melted record on it."

"That's unbelievable," said Diego. "Can I get you a piece of pizza?"

"The closest kosher pizza is fifty blocks from here," said the jeweler.

"Then when I'm rich I'll come back and buy something."

Diego took the piece from the counter, placed it back on Anna's neck and they started to leave.

"Wait, wait a minute! This could be a very valuable piece of jewelry. It could be so valuable you might not have to work for a living. Let me show it to someone who knows."

"We have to leave," said Anna.

"I have a camera here," said the jeweler. "May I take a picture and call you if you have a treasure? Whether you sell it or not, you should know the history."

"I'm not inter–"

"Let him take a picture." Diego jumped in. "I'll call him in a few weeks to find out if you should have insurance or whatever."

"She doesn't have to take it off," he continued to persist.

She nodded okay and leaned over the counter.

The jeweler took a camera from the drawer, motioned she should flip the amulet over and took a picture of the back.

"Please turn it over."

He took a second picture.

"How do I get in touch with you?" he asked again, but by that time Anna was tugging Diego to the door. "Okay, so you'll call me in a few weeks," he said, as he pressed the buzzer to unlock the door. They were halfway into the street when the jeweler called out in German, "Anna, warte, ich habe ein geschenk für dich!"

"Nein danke," she responded as the door close behind them.

The jeweler scrambled toward the back and yelled out, "Seymour!"

A boy ran out of a backroom.

The jeweler reached into his pocket and took out some cash. "Seymour, a couple is walking west on this side. She has short black hair with a pony tail, and he's shorter with an old leather jacket, brown with an airplane on the back. Follow them wherever they go and then call me. Don't let them see you. And you mustn't lose them. If they split up, follow the woman. Here's money just in case."

"Just in case what?"

"Just in case she lives in Chicago, putz. Now go!"

Seymour grabbed his coat and ran out. The jeweler looked up at the video surveillance camera to check if the light was on. He ran to the back to check if the tape was running. Then he dialed the phone.

CHAPTER 36

The super's wife knew better than to ask her husband about his plans. To do that would require admitting she heard the conversation with his new boss in the basement. She knew he would lash out about her eavesdropping instead of admitting a woman pushed him around. He was now disappearing a few hours a week, and she never asked him where he had been. The opposite of a partnership is what she had gotten herself into after marrying for security, a fast track to adulthood and a hasty departure from the doting clan she found herself surrounded by in America. After a week of marriage, she realized that he was incapable of love, and that eliminated any possibility of motherhood. No love, no children. Her copy of *The Birth Control Handbook* and her Enovid pill wheel were wrapped in a dish towel, placed behind a sterling soup terrine on the highest shelf in the kitchen. He never even noticed she wasn't having her periods. He did, however, notice she put on a few pounds and constantly complained that her breasts were too sensitive to be touched.

She lived in two worlds; one inhabited by a man she cooked, cleaned and reluctantly spread her legs for and the other, her private world inhabited by a young Latina and an old Jew.

One of the three vacant apartments were rented by white folks fleeing the brown and black 'invasion' of much of the Bronx, which had become dangerous. Abandoned tenements lined the streets of the South Bronx. The white residents who could afford or almost afford the rents had raced to Queens, Long Island and parts of the North Bronx and Riverdale. Yet, the response to the classified ad in *The Times* had dwindled to prank calls. A one and two bedroom were still available, the tenants of which had disappeared leaving behind some furniture and appliances including an Amana Radar Range. After waiting a few weeks to see if anyone came to claim anything, Rita and Izolda found a new home for it in the old man's cubicle. The old man would sit in the once derelict rocking chair listening to his station and staring at the appliance as if it just landed from Mars.

He had become Rita's diversion from having to cope with the unfriendly environment out there in the alien streets of Riverdale and her school. She would visit the withdrawn, crumpled enigma a few times a week to bring him asopao, arroz con pollo or his favorite, sopa di pollo. When it wasn't food it was a thermos of tea or Café Bustello. Working had distracted him ten hours a day for twenty-five years. Now he had to survive twenty-four hours and not fourteen and, although he preferred to be left alone, he tolerated Rita doing her homework, sitting by his shelf on a kitchen stool she lugged back and forth from her apartment. Occasionally she would ask him a homework question. Most of the time, rather than giving an answer, he would pose a question instead, the answer to which required thought that would lead her to discovering the answer on her own or something more important or useful.

"What historic figure was more important; Metternich or Lister," she asked.

"What's more important food or water?" he responded.

"Water is more important," she answered confidently.

"But what if the food has water in it?" he countered.

"How much water?" she asked.

What she was learning was that it's all like an iceberg – only 10 percent is obvious, but when one probes possibilities and goes beneath the surface, everything is more complicated and rewarding. The exercise was far more important than getting an answer.

CHAPTER 37

The old man, exhausted from doing nothing, was lying in bed when Nowicki appeared in the doorway.

"You don't have to pay next month's rent because there probably won't be a next month. The owner wants me to tear down your room. She wants you to make other arrangements. Also, throw away that wire with the loop at the end. You'll have to pay to use the machines until you leave.

The old man didn't budge, just stared at the ceiling. Nowicki headed out of the basement and up to his apartment to talk to his wife.

CHAPTER 38

Off-season business was just enough to pay Diego and Anna and make a few dollars. Local regulars came and went, but not the freezing cold. It came and stayed. Moe spent more time on the boardwalk than he did in season. He was far from antisocial, but there was a time for friends and customers and a time for him, his memories and the wonder of serenity disrupted only by the sound of crashing waves and wind challenging his earmuffs. New customers were rare and stood out. What was unusual was that a few times the same person would show up in the shop, order coffee and nurse it for longer than usual. Moe tried to engage, but the stranger had little to say. Diego had noticed that there were times Anna would show up for her shift and he would show up for a cup of coffee a few seconds later. He would nurse it for a while and leave without finishing it. After a few of these visits, Anna had also noticed his behavior and seemed to be on edge. On one occasion, he was in his car in the parking lot when Diego was about to leave for school. He had planned to be at study hall for an hour or so but decided to keep an eye on Anna and the stranger. The bus pulled away and so did the man in the car. Diego, more curious than suspicious, followed on his bike. Anna got off the bus and hurried to Moe's house.

She raced up the stairs to her window and peeked through the lace curtains. Across the street, the man pulled up, lingered a bit then drove away. She sunk to the floor below the window and stared forward. Diego followed the man until he was going too fast to keep up with.

CHAPTER 39

zolda and Rita, bundled up, sat on a park bench pondering what the future looked like and the mystery of the old man.

"He must have done something horrible or something horrible was done to him," Izolda thought aloud.

Rita shrugged.

Izolda continued. "He wasn't born this way…. Maybe he's in hiding because of something he did in Poland. Maybe he was one of those Jews who helped the Nazis."

Rita jumped in. "In shop class at school we were given a sheet of copper and a hammer with a ball at the end. We then had to hammer the copper into whatever shape we wanted. I made an ashtray. Izzie, what hammered him into who he is? And where will he go, and who will be there for him when he gets there?"

"We know he won't make new friends or ask for help," added Izolda. "It's freezing. He won't survive out here."

"And I won't survive my algebra final," moaned Rita.

They headed home.

When Izolda opened the door to her apartment, she found her husband sitting in the kitchen.

"How was your day?" she asked.

"I've been offered more respect, more pay and a nice apartment with a room for our baby. I told the old man that he has to leave and that we're leaving."

"You what?"

"You heard me. I told him he has to find somewhere else or go back to the bushes. Start putting your things together."

"But I'm happy here," his shocked wife shouted.

"You'll be just as happy a block away."

"No I won't."

"Yes you will."

"No I won't."

"How do you know?"

"Because you'll be there!"

"You are not a true Polish wife. Something must have happened to you on the boat. I made a mistake."

"No, husband, I made the mistake. I should have had you fill out an application like the tenants have to. One of the questions would have asked if you knew had to love and respect someone."

"Woman, it's not normal to not get pregnant. It's been five years and nothing."

"I made sure of that. No child deserves a father like you."

He moved to slap her, and she caught his hand.

"Husband, there's more to me than an apron, a broom and a hole between my legs. Go and find a woman who deserves you. I release you."

Nowicki grinned. "I promised my new boss I would bring him tenants from the building. He promised to keep their rent at what they're paying now. After a year, he can do what he wants with their rents. They won't want to move again. You will come to me sooner than later. You'll change your mind when this building is falling apart and half-empty. You know where to find me."

CHAPTER 40

A few nights after the incident, Diego was finishing salting the ice puddle in front of his store caused by the melting snow on the roof. Moe had left earlier. Diego returned to the rear table top strewn with books and notes and homework. He sat, put the Walkman's earbuds back in his ears, started highlighting and ingesting portions of the book in front of him when he heard banging looked up and saw that same man he followed rapping at the front door. Diego waved and shouted, "we're closed," but the stranger persisted and wouldn't stop rapping. Diego finally went to the door and screamed, "We're closed, and all the cash is in the bank already."

"I don't want your money," the man reacted. "I want to talk to you."

"About stalking Anna, you deviant?"

"I'm not a stalker, but I do want to talk to you about her."

"Get the fuck out of here or I'll call the police."

The man moved the front of his jacket to the side exposing a gun in a belt-holster. "The glass won't protect you. Close the lights and we can sit and talk in the back of the store, or

I can force you to come with me long before the police are here, and your life will change forever," he said staring holes through Diego's eyes. "All I want is information and your help. Please open the door."

Diego hesitated. "Talk to me about what?"

"About those of us who seek justice for the six million we've lost."

CHAPTER 41

Ceci and Priscilla returned to the mansion after they had checked out two flea markets and gotten the lay of the land if Ceci decided to teach a few neighbor's maids how to make karabellas, pay for a spot at a flea market and sell them to make enough bucks to pay herself for working for Priscilla Cates and hover above poverty. They sat at the kitchen table and listened to the two messages left while they were out.

The first was from Izolda:

This is Izolda Nowicki, the super's wife in Riverdale. My husband took all his things to his new building around the corner. Knowing him, he probably didn't prepare you for his leaving. He said some tenants would go with him. I'm sorry. I have decided I don't want to be married to him, and I want to stay here. I can talk to the tenants. I can't do the maintenance, but I can do everything else. I also copied all the phone numbers of the people he called in to do repairs in the building that he couldn't do. I copied their names and numbers a few days ago while he was out. I promise I'll make sure the building is rented and tell you what's going on. I hope that will be enough to stay in the apartment. I will look for a job if you want me to pay rent. I hope this is okay with you. I'm nervous but happy. He was stealing money from you and my life from me. He's torn down the room in the basement, and I can't find the old man. My friend and I took all his things to an empty apartment. Please come to the building as soon as you can. We're in apartment 3C with his things.

"That ungrateful son of a bitch, Priscilla exploded. "I—"

Ceci cut her off. "Listen to the second message. It could be the bastard."

They listened to the second message.

Ms. Cates, this is John Peterson at the bank. Please understand that I would have bent the rules a bit if there was a gray area, but if things are so tight maybe it's time to sell. I thought I'd let you know that my wife is in real estate. She's a wiz who can help you market your house. She thinks you could have enough profit to pay off the mortgage, the equity loan and the back taxes and have a bit left over for a fresh start. Also, I'm not sure if it's okay with you, and I certainly would seek your approval if it came to that, but I was serious about a real job for your assistant. Please call if I can help you both. When you dial the bank's number, select extension 11.

"Real job?" Priscilla reacted. "Does he think you're a slave? First that phony says I'm worthless and then he invites his wife to put her hand in my pocket. Was my father right, Ceci? Are all men vultures? Do they sit up on branches and hilltops ready to pounce on those below who need help?"

Cecilia leaned forward almost nose to nose.

"Lady, vultures eat carrion. Haitian vultures and men like your father and your banker are hyenas. They eat their pray dead or alive. You were raised in a vacuum and almost ruined by a predator a million miles away from the real world. When I go shopping or get gas for the car, people talk to me. They tell me that your father used goons to collect the rents, threw families and children out on the street and never fixed anything. Rats would walk across children's beds, but he didn't have to call an exterminator because his inmates had no place to go. The only proof that he had a heart is that it attacked and killed him."

"You have some nerve talking to me that way," Priscilla shouted.

Ceci fired back. "Most of the men in Haiti live in the shadows of a mob that can only feed their families by exposing others as traitors. In Haiti, a traitor is someone who has an opinion other than the boss man's. A man goes to work and disappears. No news. No nothing; just a family that's going to starve. Children roam the streets looking for a parent who was one of the 50,000 slaughtered by our president for life. A thousand miles away from here and your bullshit problems my good father, mother and sister have been dropped into a black hole, and I know that I'll never see them again. You're like a clam that never opened, and you know what happens to them; sooner than later they get thrown away."

Priscilla Cates looked away.

Ceci sat there for a minute or so, put her hands on her boss's shoulders and turned her around.

Priscilla spoke before she could say anything. "Please don't be mad at me. I couldn't pick and choose the father I wanted. Mine came with the house. My mother bailed out when I was eleven, and I was totally dependent on him, but I'm not like him. Believe me, I can get things done without being like him."

"I'm not the person you have to convince, boss lady, you are. You did just fine when you confronted that asshole in Riverdale."

"I don't know where that came from, but it felt good…and I couldn't have done it without you next to me. I enjoyed being that person and being in the Bronx. I liked all the scents of the city instead of smelling salt water day after day. I don't know why I'm not on the floor in the fetal position, but I'm not."

"You're on your way," said Cecilia. You won't need me sooner than you think."

"What I think is that we could make good partners."

"Is that right, Ms. Cates? So you're ready to go fifty-fifty with a woman as black as night?"

"You might be black as night, but wherever you go and whatever you say; you fill the place with light…. And who said it was fifty-fifty?"

Ceci stiffened up, crossed her arms, squinted and tilted her head in disapproval waiting for a response.

"You drive a hard bargain," reacted Priscilla as she extended her hands. Ceci took them both in hers.

"Let's go to the building and kick some ass."

They hugged.

"Where are we going to stay?" Ceci continued.

"What do you mean?"

"Partner, straightening things out could take days or weeks, and I don't think we should use what's left of your fortune to pay for a flea bag in the Bronx."

"Then let's take some bedding and sleep in the vacant apartment. I know the landlord. She won't charge us for staying there."

"I can't wait to see you sleeping on a floor." Ceci giggled.

"For some reason I'm not nervous," Priscilla thought out loud. "I'll drive."

"Now I'm nervous," reacted Ceci. "What about the old man?" she continued.

"What about him?" asked Priscilla.

"Who'll be handling his situation, you or your father?"

An hour later, bags, clothing and assorted necessities sat on the back seat of a car revving in anticipation while Priscilla Cates held the wheel and craned her neck waiting at the end of the entrance ramp until there were no cars in sight before getting on a highway for the first time in her life.

"Are you sure you want to drive?" asked Ceci.

"Never surer," the hyper-focused daughter of Murray Cates responded.

Ceci sat next to her staring forward, straight-backed, clutching her wooden cross to her chest.

CHAPTER 42

The old man sat against the window in the last row of a bus he'd never been on. Two filled shopping bags hugged against his chest sat on his lap. He had no idea where he was going or what he would do when he got there. He scanned the advertising that lined the concave intersection of the sides and roof of the bus. He looked at the assortment of people standing, sitting, getting on and off. Fordham Road was swamped with cars. The bus was gridlocked in the middle of the Grand Concourse, the Bronx's Park Avenue. A poorly taken care of grass, mostly dirt, median ended just below his window. A derelict in rags, legs splayed and dirt crusted feet exposed, sat comma-posed against a troubled tree. The old man couldn't take his eyes off him. Their eyes met. The derelict bent forward extended his hands up toward him. It was as if the old man's fate was beckoning. The bus moved on and filled up, standing room only. He offered his seat to a pregnant woman, a ten-ish year-old girl hanging on her arm. He rose, the shopping bags held to his chest. The lady thanked him and sat. The girl sitting on mom's lap looked up at him.

"You're a nice man," she said, smiling.

When the bus lurched forward, he and the bags fell on top of them. The girl started laughing until she saw what was under the T-shirt that no longer covered the contents of one of the bags. Her eyes widened. She stared in the bag for a moment then quickly placed the shirt back on top and looked up.

"Mister, you're not a good stander. I think you should sit, and we should stand."

He looked down at her, nodded a thank you and left the bus at the next stop. After he got off he looked back.

Her nose pressed against the window, she was waving goodbye with one hand and a thumb up on the other. The old man sat on the bus stop bench. He watched as the bus crawled out of sight and disappeared in traffic.

CHAPTER 43

The Atlantic Beach Bridge was empty except for the couple glistening with sweat, elbows on the rail, facing southeast along the inlet, out to the Atlantic, the end of the Far Rockaway Boardwalk and the beaches. They were fine physical specimens for a couple in their sixties. Age, oppressive heat, rain, sleet, freezing cold and a few Nor'easters had been no deterrents to their morning three mile race starting on the beach that abutted their bungalow rental. They always ran the same pattern – a fifty-yard sprint after jogging each couple of hundred yards. The race ended at the middle of the Atlantic Beach Bridge where they would take off their twin backpacks, remove the powerful Swift LandScope from one and the tripod from the other and set them up. As the powerful ocean currents sprinted beneath them through the narrowing channel rushing from the ocean into Reynolds Channel and Long Island's Great South Bay, the land scope didn't budge for the entire time.

A year ago, the nature lovers had impressed Martha, owner of Martha's Manors, to rent one of her summer bungalows year-round. Their rental application and passports showed they were French Canadians although they didn't sound like the French Canadian couple that rented one of Martha's places on Lido Beach every summer. They asked and received permission to use a rented space heater for the winter, but barely used it. They also agreed to pay a portion of the extra insurance needed to protect Martha during the off-season months. Wherever they came from, they had traveled light. Only a few pieces of outerwear hung in the closet and there were drawers left almost empty after they put their duffels and clothing away.

Martha had been left with a dozen or so summer rental bungalows from Lido Beach to the Rockaways by her husband who had a heart attack on the beach after fighting a massive striped bass from the shore. He dropped dead while holding up the catch of a lifetime. His last thought must have been, 'You weren't worth it.'

Martha was left with no bills, mortgages or children. The couple paid their rent on time. With the exception of their daily run and a drive into Far Rockaway almost every day they rarely left the area. Martha couldn't grasp why they wanted to spend their days and nights during the off season on a street with no occupants and a beach that was desolate. Extra income was always welcomed, and they were a pleasant, sophisticated couple.

CHAPTER 44

Izolda and Rita had combed the bushes around their side of the park and had only sweat and scrapes to show for it. They checked alleys and basements. They went downtown to Berkowitz. The name on the building register was being changed to Hong and Son. They stopped by the breakfast place. Nothing.

"Where would he go?"

"He can't have gotten very far."

"But in what direction?"

"He's probably doing better that we are," moaned Rita. "I'm exhausted and I want to go home."

They left downtown, ascended the subway steps and walked the few blocks to the building. Priscilla and Ceci were leaning back against her car and didn't move after they saw the couple approach, Priscilla's expression showed her dissatisfaction.

"I'm Priscilla Cates. I'm guessing by the expression on your face and the name on your jean's jacket that you are Mr. Nowicki."

"I'm sorry," reacted Izolda. "This was my husband's jacket. We were looking for the old man. We looked everywhere."

"We looked everywhere for you too," said Ceci.

"There should always be someone in the building for emergencies," said Priscilla.

"This *is* an emergency," said Rita. "An old man who just got over pneumonia, who has no money, family, friends or job was kicked out of the building by you. He's on the streets somewhere, and he's a human not a leak under a sink!"

"Rita, don't be rude!" shouted Izolda.

"Let's start over with introductions. I'm Priscilla Cates, and this is my partner, Cecilia Papouloute. Please call me Priscilla and she likes 'Ceci.'"

"I'm Izolda Nowicki and this is Rita Ruiz, apartment 4A. She calls me Izzie."

"Rita," said Priscilla, "I didn't tell him to throw the old man out. I told him to make other arrangements."

"I heard you say 'this is not a shelter,'" said Rita.

"It's not, but I wasn't aware Izzie's husband is a heartless son of a bitch."

"Son of a bitch isn't fair," said Ceci. "We don't know the mother. Heartless piece of crap sounds right."

"You really don't know where the old man is?" asked Priscilla.

"No."

"Did you call the police?"

Rita mimicked a dismissive policeman on the phone.

"Lady, I'm sorry about the old man. I'm also sorry about the one or two thousand other missing old men. Does he have the Alzheimer's?"

"I told him that he's as sharp as we are," said Izolda.

"All I can do is get a description, and you can get on line with the others," said the policeman. "Come down to the station." He hung up.

"I want to see the basement," said Priscilla. "And then we'll talk about the building and the old man."

"And we'll talk about me?" asked Izolda.

"We will," answered her boss.

Izolda continued, "Four more tenants asked if they leave will their security deposit cover the last month's rent. I'm really worried."

Cecilia jumped in, "Worry is one option. Action is another."

CHAPTER 45

Not only did Alexander's Department store influence the intersection of The Grand Concourse and Fordham road, it influenced what millions of middle-class Bronxites wore for decades. The men's clothing section was on the first floor toward the rear. A six-inch oak platform and a tailor waiting for his next cuff or sleeve shortening sat in the center of the ring of dressing rooms. Burlap curtains on rods provided the privacy all expected. It was a slow day. Only one curtain was closed.

"Are you okay in there?" the tailor asked heading toward the dressing room. No answer. He asked again. The curtain opened, and the old man, holding his vest, walked out wearing a plaid sports shirt, a cardigan, and a pair of pants that needed shortening and cuffs. The tailor pinned his cuffs, advised him that the pants would be ready in an hour. He asked the tailor to watch his things and he'd be back in less than an hour. He took his vest with him, headed for the luggage department, bought a small suitcase, then went back to the dressing room and closed the curtain. A few minutes later, he emerged carrying the suitcase, left the curtain opened and advised the tailor that he didn't have to watch his belongings any longer and would be back to pick up his pants. He left Alexanders walked to the other side of Fordham Road and went into Gorman's Hot Dogs, had two and an orange drink, returned to Alexanders. After putting on his new pants and belt he asked the tailor to throw away the ratty gabardine ones he'd been wearing as long as he could remember. Aaron thanked him and headed to the shoe department carrying the suitcase. The salesman suggested wingtips. The old man said, "I want to walk not fly." As he left the store again, he looked at himself in the mirror-lined entryway. He nodded his approval, walked to an eastbound bus stop, boarded a bus, transferred once and ended up in front of E.J. Korvette's Department Store. He was in there for twenty minutes and walked out pleased with his discovery. His agenda complete, he headed back across the Bronx to Riverdale, the apartment building and the clearing in Van Cortlandt Park in case he needed it.

CHAPTER 46

Diego had not gotten a good night's sleep since he let the man into the shop and sat there listening to him in the dark for over three hours. Until that encounter, the only drama in his life had been waiting to see grades posted and whether the Knick's would make the playoffs again. His world was upside down now. He had received an education about The Italian Red Cross and the Vatican's participation in aiding many of the over one hundred thousand high ranking Nazi's and collaborators from all over Europe to evade justice via something called 'the rat line,' a series of safe havens along an escape route system through Italy, Spain and Scandinavia that relocated Nazis and sympathizers over the globe, to Australia, Canada and mostly to South American countries that were run by dictators, particularly Argentina. He had listened in the dark, with eyes shut, about his own country's vomiting up visas to and hoarding dozens of Nazis and suspected Nazis that could be of use during the post war years regardless of their direct and indirect participation in crimes against his country and humanity. He listened to the prima facie evidence that Anna's mother and father were among the worst of the worst. Although he wasn't sure whether or not she knew she had been knee deep in evil and if she could and would provide useful information, the passionate stranger was convinced that sooner or later this child of The Reich would be contacted by her mother and father or someone else thus laying bare a path to heinous criminals who must be exposed and punished.

Diego had sat there stunned, his simple, innocent life altered forever. At the end of that presentation, he had received his marching orders. He was given a small tin box filled with wax to imprint Anna's house key. He would alert the Nazi hunter when the house would be vacant for at least six hours and record unusual activity. He would record the visits by strangers, especially the man and woman in their SS uniforms on the front page clip out from *The San Antonio Press News*. The hunter insisted he memorize their faces and not be fooled by a beard or by their hair color or style. The hunter finished with: "To follow these instructions could guarantee a normal life for Anna regardless of what she knows and be forever appreciated by good people, victims, the family of victims all over the world and would, in the eyes of God, be a mitzvah. However, if you choose not to engage, all bets are off. That includes a bet on your girlfriend escaping a storm that would wash her and her life away."

Diego didn't need time to think. The first words out of his mouth had advised the hunter that this coming Sunday Moe's reward for his acing his finals and Anna making all the glassware sparkle like polished crystal, was a day on the town including three decent seats at the Knick/Celtic game. The three of them would be gone all day and most of the night. In season, Moe would never take off on a Sunday, but when snow was on the ground, his buddies Vinny and Anna Stancati could open, close and take good care of customers when Moe took the rare day off. Moe reciprocated by taking care of their grocery store for a day here and there. The hunter told him where to leave the key imprint and added, "If you allow her to use your phone we'll be listening. If you must make personal calls use the one here or a payphone."

"Anything else?" had asked Diego with an attitude.

"You are not a Jew. You might have second thoughts. If you do, remember this: Picture her father sitting at a desk in the square at a train station deciding whether the Jewish man, woman or child in front of him would be gassed, taken into the woods and shot or worked to death. Hear the screaming as the ones who were too sick or too old or too young were not allowed to board, separated from their loved ones and trucked away. Picture those lucky ones digging mass graves they were shoved down into to be machine gunned and buried. Picture his wife, the woman next to him in the picture, sitting at a table supervising other heartless women behind several rows of long tables that were covered with the contents of the crammed valises and bags of those who boarded the train or trucks and were forced to leave their belongings behind. Picture her and those under her command sorting their personal posses-sions into bins of precious metal to be melted, articles that were needed, items that had value and junk as their previous owners, scared to death, were on the way to starvation and the furnaces. See the thousands of pictures of husbands and wives, grandfathers, grandmothers and children going up in smoke as most of the victims would in a few days. Picture his wife, a proud smile on her face knowing it had been a good day."

The hunter rose and left. Diego had sat in the dark for ten minutes, then turned the lights on and looked down at the table. On it was a business card with only a telephone number and the tin of wax. A few days later, the hunters had the duplicate key and were ready for Sunday.

CHAPTER 47

Martha rarely checked up on adult renters without children, especially seniors, but as she drove on Beach Boulevard on the way to the supermarket passed her only rented bungalow, she noticed the front door was opened and it was dark inside. She slowed down, parked, walked to the door, rapped on the open door's glass pane then walked inside. The place was empty, and there was no trace anyone had ever been there.

CHAPTER 48

"I'd like to see an apartment," said the nicely dressed older gentleman to the lady in the temporary rental office.

"Do you have a family?"

"Of course. My wife is working. There's only the two of us.

She took him to the third floor and walked him through the one-bedroom model apartment. He followed her around without observing or listening to what she said until they were back at her desk.

"All apartments have central air, spacious closets and a laundry room on each floor. Each floor has a laundry room with washers and dryers and a sorting table."

"How many washers and dryers are there on a floor?" he asked.

"There are three of each on a floor," she answered, proudly.

"And how many tenants are there on a floor?"

"Sixteen to twenty."

"And how much does it cost to do a wash?"

"It costs a quarter per wash or dry."

"So if you have two washes it would cost one dollar."

She looked him over and smiled.

"I'm sure you can handle it. We have a few two bedrooms available at the moment. Would you like to see one?"

"No, thank you."

"Do you have a superintendent managing the building?"

"We have one here," she answered. "The other building has a professional management company a phone call away.

"I like that," he said.

"So do our tenants."

"Not all superintendents are easy to get along with," he added.

"Absolutely," she agreed.

"But you have a superintendent here," he said, acting concerned.

"I wouldn't worry about that." She winked.

"How long can a lease be?"

"One year."

"What about the other building?"

"I can walk you over there or you can look at the plan on the wall."

"How many tenants on a floor over there?"

"Twenty."

"And the same laundry room?"

"Exactly."

He thanked her again and started to leave.

"Apartments are going fast, and over three-quarters of both buildings are rented," she cautioned. "Don't you want to know about the rent? May I have your name?" she called out to his back, but he was yards away headed for the front door and home.

CHAPTER 49

The sky was robin's egg blue. The clouds had decided to give New York a rest and visit the cities to the west. The freezing Manhattan was swarming with life. Silvery vapor from mouths and noses glistened, back-lighted by a sun thankful it could provide some warmth for its fans. It had been a long day starting with the flea market on Columbus at eight and ending in pretty good seats at the vibrating Madison Square Garden. The day had been packed with so many divertissements including blintzes at the Russian Tea Room, a Reuben at Reuben's and a stroll up Orchard Street and around the Lower Eastside ending at Katz's Deli where, unlike the usable prize in a box of crackerjacks, Anna discovered her unusable prize, a fried cockroach, in her fries. She was having the time of her life, a rare day not tethered to her past or thoughts of her past. This was proof she could be like anyone else and enjoy the freedom and treasures available to normal people who were living their lives in the present, people making memories not drowning in them. Neither the Nazi hunter walking a few yards behind the threesome nor anyone else noticed the separated pair parallel to them on the other side of the street – the same man and woman who were on the Atlantic Beach Bridge. They walked back and forth with no continuous pattern when Anna, Moe and Diego stopped to window shop. Separated by thirty or forty yards, each had a tiny pair of opera glasses and had close up views of Anna several times until she entered The Garden. The couple used the glasses only when surrounded by one of the continuous clusters of pedestrians streaming by in waves, some escaping the current peeling off onto one of the endless rivulets of streets leaving the human river and making their way to thousands of destinations. Anna was also oblivious to the man following her and entering The New York Knickerbockers' home.

For Diego, who had been a frustrated Knick fan since birth, the reward for good grades was very special. For now, the encounter with that intruder was pushed to the back of his mind. The Knicks had finally won a NBA championship in May and were defending it. During the game, whenever he wasn't standing and screaming, Diego tried and failed to teach Anna about basketball basics. Moe sat there with a smile on his face observing them more than the game.

Sylvia, he thought to himself, I'm so sorry my lousy sperm count cost us what we were born for.

Anna left her seat twice, once for a bathroom break, the other for some water. Both times she thought a familiar face sitting a few rows behind her had left his seat as she passed and returned when she did. But the day was too grand to think those thoughts. Leaving the sunshine to return to the dark was out of the question.

CHAPTER 50

There were four of them wearing gloves, hats and mittens on their shoes. The hunt started in the only closet in Anna's room. One hunter checked out two pairs of shoes, a shoe box, an empty duffle bag and other unremarkable items on the floor. The other checked all the hems and linings of the one heavy jacket and several other light ones. He checked the few blouses dresses, skirts and jeans. He did so with his eyes, his fingers feeling for paper or other objects and his ears listening for the usual crinkling sound made by something between the lining and outer fabric. His back against the closet's back wall, he checked the opposite closet wall, above the door jam, the back of the door, the ceiling and found nothing. He left the closet, looked back, double-checked everything and returned the door to slightly open. The other hunter had finished bugging the downstairs phone and was installing a second bug in the upstairs one. After he finished, he placed a bug on the underside of the base of the lamp next to the bed. The third hunter looked over the wrought iron bed stand and lamp, checked behind the radiator and under the window air conditioning unit. The small chest of drawers was next. Each drawer was opened, contents inspected including the back and underside. He lay down on the floor and looked under the chest using his flashlight. Not satisfied, he returned to the closet for a wire hanger he swept back and forth under the chest to reach areas he couldn't see and then opted to remove the few things from the top and tilt the whole piece to see its underside and back. Once done, he made sure the contents of the drawers were back in their original position. He looked at the bed. It was the remaining object in the room. He memorized the position of the bedding and placed it all beside the bed. They checked the pillows and comforter. There was nothing between the mattress and box spring. They checked the seams of the mattress and box spring to see if they had been ripped and resewn. One went to the other side of the bed, turned on his flashlight, lay down to inspect the underside of the box spring. The beige letter-sized manila envelope was wedged between the bottom of the box spring and the center slat that supported it. He inched under the bed until he positioned himself to fist up the box spring and slide the envelope onto his chest. No tape was used to seal the envelope; only the usual string and a paper button protected Anna from who knows what, from who knows whom and the misery. Still on his back, he handed the envelope to another cohort who took the envelope downstairs to the kitchen table, carefully opened it, spread out the contents, took a Minox mini-camera from his pocket, photographed everything, put the contents back in the envelope, wound the string back around the paper button, tied it and took it back upstairs. The same man, still positioned on his back, slid back under the bed and repositioned the envelope between the slat and the bottom of the box spring.

They all went downstairs to wait for the cover of darkness to leave.

"I have to give it to these Nazis," one of them said. "If that maniac was as careful and intelligent as these two, they would have won the war.

CHAPTER 51

The three women and teenage girl sat around the kitchen table of the Nowicki apartment. A few assorted cakes, crumbs and an empty pot of coffee on a trivet sat on top of the flower-print oil cloth covering the table.

"Enough is enough. We're not sitting at a table under Vesuvius having coffee during an eruption! Enough about the problems," shouted Cecilia. Let's talk solutions."

"Which problem do we solve first?" asked Rita.

"The immediate problem is cash flow. Our property insurance is coming due," answered Cecilia.

"What about the old man?" asked Izolda.

"We'll figure something out," Priscilla answered.

"You promise?" asked Rita and Izolda at the same time.

"We'll figure something out, but for now, how do we keep our tenants?"

That won't be a problem," said the old man from the doorway to the kitchen. I need you to give me the architectural plans of the building, and I also have to see one apartment in each column to make sure that all of them have the same layout."

Izolda said, "There are only two layouts in the whole building."

"Do all have the same entry layout, kitchen and hallway as this one and mine?"

"Yes. The only difference is at the end of the hallway. There's either one or two bedrooms at the end, but the fronts of the apartments are exactly the same."

The old man went into the hallway and studied the space on the other side of the kitchen wall. Then he went to his apartment without saying goodbye.

CHAPTER 52

They had just descended the stairs of The Long Island Railroad's Arverne station.

"That was one hell of a day," blurted Diego. "You guys brought the Knicks luck. A thirty-foot shot that went in off the backboard is nothing but luck, and it won the game. Moe, thanks for a hell of a day. I think I have a Jewish ancestor. What else could be the reason I ate so many blitzes?"

"That's blintzes," reacted Moe. "It has an 'n' in it."

"No wonder it tastes so good. Anna, hop on my bike, and I'll give you a lift home."

"What about me?" asked Moe.

"What about you? You're parked in front of the store."

"I'm joking. I'm joking," he reacted and turned toward Anna. "I want to check out the shop. I'll be home in a half-hour unless you want to walk with me to the shop, and I'll drive us home."

"I'm tired," said Anna. "I'll go with Diego."

"Moe," said Anna already on the bike. "Please take this." She handed him a folded piece of paper and whispered, "Go," to Diego.

As he started to pedal away, Diego called back, "Moe, the next day on the town is my treat. Maybe we'll take the Gentile tour."

Moe unfolded the piece of paper and read it:

> *Thank you for saving me*
> *Thank you for believing in me.*
> *Thank you for the job.*
> *Thank you for trusting me*
> *Thank you for everything*
> > *Your Anna*
> *PS: I'm happy I seem to be helping to clean your beach*
> *a little after all.*

Both exhausted and exhilarated when she got to her room, she sat at the edge of her bed smiling, then walked over to the closet door and opened it. Anna looked at herself in the door mirror. She looked different, more relaxed, younger. She turned and faced the bed. The only connection to the old Anna was under the center of her bed wedged between the box spring and a slat. She dropped to her knees, lied back, slid a few inches under the bed, groped around, found and removed the envelope.

Anna wanted one more look at the newspaper clippings before she burned them and her memories in the bathtub. She tried to unwind the string around the paper button, but it was knotted. A chill ran up her spine, and she started to wring her hands and vibrate. The glorious day evaporated. Once again the old urge to take off for who knows where returned.

CHAPTER 53

They sat in Izolda's kitchen watching him pour over the building's floor and apartment layouts.

The old man looked up at Priscilla. "You are sure that nothing has been changed since the building was built?"

"Nothing, for the tenth time," replied Priscilla, impatiently.

"And each floor is the same?" he asked.

"Yes, again," Ceci answered, perturbed.

He kept looking at Priscilla, his elbows on the table, his palms pressed against his temples. "Are you even familiar with the floor plans of your building?" He chided.

"I've been on another planet," she reacted. "I'm here now and will do what I should have done after my father died. I know what you think of me and that's going to change. In a few days, Ceci and I will know everything about this place. Are you or aren't you going to tell us what you're thinking?"

"Do you trust your plumber and carpenter?" he asked Izolda.

"It's my husband's plumbers and carpenters."

Priscilla sprung up. "What are you talking about? Tell me what you're thinking about God damn it!"

Ceci took her arm and pulled her back to the seat. "I suspect that behind what's left of his blue eyes, he's thinking about the solution."

"THE SOLUTION!?" screamed Priscilla. "The new buildings are nicer and have more to offer. We're losing tenants, and last but not least, the building is what it is, and I'm broke."

They sat there for a while until the old man spoke. "I will tell you how you will keep your tenants and have a waiting list of new ones even though you raise your rents a little, but only after I eat something and you promise me a one-bedroom apartment, rent free, until I die, and that you will all leave me alone until then. When I die, there will be no funeral. You will cremate me. I can only hope that after I share the fate of most of the people I knew and those I loved, there will be no after life only oblivion and peace."

Rita sprang up. "What awful thing have you done? What horror has made you be like this, live like this? Are you or are you not a monster?" She ran out of the room.

"Do we have a deal?" he persisted.

"Sure," Ceci answered. But we can't promise you there's no afterlife or oblivion."

"After I eat something, I'll tell you my plan," he said matter-of-factly. "Someone go check on her."

Ceci turned toward Izolda, "Maybe I can make a Haitian meal. May I check out the kitchen?"

"You must be kidding? That'll take all day," reacted her partner. "Give him a sandwich. Do you have hard boiled eggs or tuna fish?" Priscilla asked Izolda.

"Both," she answered.

"I like egg salad with some chopped onion and pepper," he said.

"Good," said Priscilla. "Have a sandwich with chopped onion and pepper and then save us, Mr. ... I don't know your name."

"My name is Aaron Luckman. And are my terms acceptable to you too?"

"My partner said they are. So they are."

Rita, wiping her eyes with a piece of toilet paper, walked back in and sat.

"I don't have bread," said Izolda.

"Rita will get some," he said.

It was the first time the old man said her name.

He reached into his pocket, took out a bill, gently took Rita's wrist and placed a fifty on her palm.

"Go get some rye bread with no seeds, please."

They all stared at the fifty and then him.

"Sorry, it's all I have."

"You won't save us until I get back, right?" moaned Rita.

"I'm hungry. Go," he ordered.

CHAPTER 54

Moe had gotten to bed at twelve or so. Just after four in the morning he heard the noises from the kitchen. He put on his robe and slippers and tiptoed across the hallway to check on Anna. Her door was open. Her closet door was open. The drawers in her chest of drawers were on her bed. He rushed down the stairs and into the kitchen. The light was on. Anna, wearing her jacket, sat at the opposite head of the kitchen table. A duffel bag leaned against the table leg. Anna had pen to paper when Moe appeared.

"What's going on?" he asked. "Where are you going?"

She kept staring at the pen and paper.

"Anna what's going on?"

She looked up. "I am going on," she answered without emotion. She looked up. Her face was frozen, her eyes smaller and darker. She looked older.

"This is your home, Anna. Have I said something, done something to make you unhappy?"

"I'm a waste of your time, Moe."

"What about the note you handed to me? What in God's name happened between last night and now?"

No response.

"Read to me what you're writing."

"I wanted to write something, but yesterday's note said it all. There was nothing left to say."

"What are you running from?"

She picked up the envelope from the table. "Do you know what this is?"

"It's an envelope," he answered.

"Have you been in my room?"

"I take the towels from the hamper when I do a wash."

"You never looked under my bed?"

"Why would I do that?"

"Someone did."

"No one has been in this house, but you and me."

"I think someone's been all over every inch of this house."

"Why? Why would anyone break in here and look under your bed?"

"Welcome to my world," said Anna.

"Your world?"

"This has been a wonderful vacation, but my world caught up with me."

"Anna, what has keeping all this inside done for you? You were miserable when I found you, and now you're miserable again."

"You'll hate me, Moe. I don't want you to hate me."

"How can I hate you, Anna? I don't care if you killed someone. You belong here. You belong in my life."

Anna collapsed onto the table sobbing.

"Let me make us some breakfast."

"No."

"Stop crying. If you trust me, you'll tell me what's going on. You owe me that. Anna, you owe me that."

A long moment passed. Without lifting her head off the table she murmured, "Make me lox, eggs and onions again, and we'll see."

CHAPTER 55

The old man finished his sandwich and nursed his cup of tea. All eyes were on him.

"You chew a lot," said Priscilla. "Do we have to wait until you finish the tea?"

He disregarded her question and asked his own. "Do any of you know a construction person you can trust?"

"My whole family is in construction," said Rita. "They work on skyscrapers and apartment buildings all over the city. My father is a project leader."

"Does he work with permits?"

"All he does is curse the city. I guess it means he works with permits."

"What about making plans to submit for approval?"

"He and his architects and draftsmen spend half their nights preparing plans for approval."

"When can I meet him?"

"He comes home for dinner about seven."

"Then we can meet tonight."

"I don't know if—"

"*If* isn't good," interrupted the old man. "The new buildings have no noisy air conditioners in the window that only cool the room they're in. There are washers and dryers on every floor. Just tell your father that it's a very big job."

"I want to know what's going on in your head," blurted Priscilla, "I want to know what the hell you're talking about, now!"

Aaron turned to her. "I don't want you to be disappointed if it's impossible."

"I'm a big girl. Let me worry about that."

A moment passed before he spoke.

"Ladies, what do you think tenants would want more than a meeting room or central air conditioning? What improvement could you give them or offer to a new tenant that would make central air conditioning and meeting rooms meaningless by comparison?"

There was no answer.

"Do you know that there's no super in one of the buildings? Tenants have to call a management company if water is pouring out of broken plumbing in the kitchen and flooding the apartment."

"Is that all you got?" a disappointed Rita moaned.

"It's just the appetizer, isn't it, Mr. Luckman?" said Ceci.

The old man continued, "No one answered my question, so listen and think: Think of your advertisements and talks with prospective tenants. Here is an example.

"In the other buildings in the neighborhood and the rest of the Bronx, tenants have to pay to wash their clothes with the clothes of neighbor's and strangers. Soiled underwear from old people and infants washed in the same machine as your underwear, your children's clothes, and everything else. Healthy people are waiting in line for sick people to finish washing their clothes and then have to pay to wash their own clothes in the same machine. The sheets that strangers sweat on, pee on and leave other stains on are washed in the same machine as yours. And, no one knows if the temperature of the hot water is high enough to kill germs. People who live in their own home don't let the whole neighborhood use their washer and dryer. And if my plan can happen, neither will your tenants. They won't have to go into a laundry room in the middle of the night because the machines were busy. They would have something no other renter in the city has – a real home. Do you think they would pay more rent if they didn't have to feed money to those machines or share them?"

"A washing machine and dryer in every apartment?" an excited Izolda thought out loud.

"Not exactly, said the old man. A company called Bendix makes one machine that washes and dries. I saw it at Korvette's Department Store. And, no vent is needed for the dryer. The plumbing and the city are another story."

"Every apartment? A washer/dryer in every apartment?" Priscilla repeated, incredulous.

He nodded.

"And who pays for these?" she continued.

"First things first." he answered.

"And do you have any idea what a job like that would cost?" asked Ceci. "My partner couldn't qualify for a $2000 loan to patch her roof."

"Jesus, Cecilia," blurted Priscilla, "that's no one's business."

"Partner," reacted Ceci. "We are all in the same 'business."

"I'll know more after tonight's meeting," said the old man. "What is more important is if it's possible. If it isn't, I don't know."

The ladies sat at the table and looked at each other.

"Rita, tell your father that I'll be waiting for him in this apartment," said the old man.

"Do you mind if we're at the meeting?" asked Rita.

"You won't be."

"I own the building. We're going to be there," Priscilla said.

"It will all be construction things, and I must learn enough to feel confident that they can do it and what it will cost. I also must know how they're doing it so I know if they're doing a good job every day. They must answer my questions without having others from anyone else. As soon as I'm convinced it's the right thing to do and it's possible to do it, we will sit down and go over everything for your approval."

CHAPTER 56

Anna, head down, had finished everything on her plate and was on her second cup of coffee. Not one word had been spoken until Moe spoke as he put the dishes and pan in the sink.

"Now it's your turn, Anna. Whatever you tell me will never be told to anyone else."

"Yes it will. If I tell you I'll probably be telling them. I don't care anymore, but please don't tell Diego."

She looked around the room, "Do you hear me! This has to end!"

Moe sat there puzzled, looked around at what she was looking at, looked back at her.

After a minute or so, she reached for the envelope but didn't open it. He placed his chair near her on the other side of the table corner and waited. She extended her hand and gently held his wrist.

"You shouldn't have gotten involved in my life."

"Too late," he came back.

"You could have problems because of me."

"Nothing will be as bad as my problems before you."

"I'm afraid you might change your mind about me."

"Only if you killed my wife."

"You mustn't tell Diego."

"Talk to me."

She fidgeted a bit and sat back. A long minute passed.

"I barely remember Bariloche or being schooled at home," she said, "but I can remember every minute of the first day in school in Mendoza when I was six. We had moved there when I was four. I don't remember the move, but I must have been unhappy about leaving my friends. The new school was fancy. Many of the children were from somewhere else and spoke many languages. My parents were born in Switzerland. They met, fell in love, got married and had me in Bariloche after settling there. My mother was a KLM stewardess who gave up her job when we moved to Mendoza. My father was an architect and engineer. They both worked all over the world and decided 'to smell the roses,' my father used to say. Spanish and English were the household languages, but our housemaid in Mendoza was German, so we spoke some German also. I was six and having a wonderful time.

My parents taught me so much about boats and hiking and so much more. They wanted me to grow up to be an independent and strong woman, and I loved them. I had so many friends in our neighborhood, and it seemed like my parents were very popular even though they didn't leave the house much. We were a threesome. We had marvelous picnics at beautiful lakes in the mountains. I learned how to sail, drive a power boat and fish. I wasn't seven yet. He even took me hunting. I killed a rabbit once and have regretted it ever since. We played sports. We ran for miles, the three of us. It was like living in an amusement park. I wasn't seven yet, but I felt like a grown up. They rarely went on vacation, just the two of them. We had many gatherings at home. It was like the United Nations. There was an occasional meeting at our home at night with only men."

She took a deep breath.

"A few times, after my mother and I went to bed, I would tiptoe downstairs and try to listen to what they were talking about. But the door was too thick to hear anything. One night the door opened when I had my ear to it. My father was very easy going but not that night. He carried me upstairs, put me down on my bed and asked if I heard anything. I told him I didn't. He kissed my forehead and pulled my cover up to my chin. 'Be a good girl and please don't do that again,' he told me.

"The next day, my mother explained that these meetings were very important to my father. They would argue about politics and whether they should invest their money or go into the wine or oil business. She also explained that sometimes they disagreed and used impolite language he didn't want me to hear. I never did it again."

Anna rubbed her temples and squinted her head ached.

"Please get me a glass of water."

Moe rose, hurried to the sink and returned with a glass full.

She gulped it down then continued, emotionless.

"Moe, I don't want you to hate me. I don't want anyone to hate me."

"Keep talking," he said.

"My eighth birthday party was a surprise sleepover with a few of my friends at my best friend, Gertie Olafson's house. It was the first time in my memory that my mother and father didn't tuck me in and say goodnight. Mrs. Olafson took me to school the next day, and I took the bus home when school was over. I got off the school bus and walked to my house as usual. The Olafsons were standing on my porch. When I was near them, Mrs. Olafson took me in her arms and hugged me to her chest. I pulled away. They took me inside and sat me down. They told me my parents had made a quick decision to drive south to look at a winery for sale and had a terrible accident on the motorway. I was afraid to ask how they were. I just sat there in hysterics. I finally asked when they would be home. They told me they wouldn't. I collapsed. Eventually I sat up and demanded to see them.

Mr. Olafson told me that there had been a fire, and there was nothing left to see. I remember that I couldn't stop shaking.

The rest is a blur except for my nightmares. The crash, the flames, their screams were not a blur. I would shake and try to catch my breath. My knuckles would get white from gripping the blanket until I took the pillow off my face, got up and went to school."

Moe rose, stepped behind Anna, hugged her around her neck and shoulders, kissed her head. She was vibrating. "My poor girl."

Anna gestured he sit back down.

"I lived with the Olafson's until I was ten. They were okay. One morning, I woke up, and they were gone just like my father and mother. No one knew anything. They took Gertie but left furniture and clothes behind, left pots and pans in the sink and disappeared. I lived in various homes until I was thirteen. I was impossible to get along with. I left school every other day until they all had enough of me.

I ended up in a place for difficult orphans in Buenos Aires. I was in and out of there until I was sixteen when I ran away. There was not enough continent south so I headed north. I was a bad girl in every way. I hitched in return for favors, I bused and walked and drank and smoked and was loose in every way. I had no one. I had been let down by everyone I loved and trusted, and so I loved and trusted no one until you and Diego. I don't have those nightmares anymore. They ended in Veracruz. They were replaced by new ones because of this."

She took a folded newspaper page out of the envelope placed it in front of him with her hand over it.

"I was hanging around in Veracruz on the way to wherever the next truck or car was headed when I stopped for some beer and cigarettes. I was in the checkout line opposite a newspaper and magazine rack. People on line were grabbing copies of La Prensa. I heard the lady in front of me say Ay, Dios mia, Oh my God."

Anna unfolded the page and placed it in front of Moe.

Moe, transfixed, stared at the image that covered most of the page.

"I'll translate," said Anna, She read the headline. "The Couple From Hell Disappears Again." She translated the sub-heading.

"They escape minutes before FGR and FBI agents carried out a nighttime raid by land and sea on their houseboat in Vera Cruz."

The proud couple on the front page in their SS uniforms stared up at Moe and Anna.

Anna gestured the introduction. "Moe, I want to introduce you to my loving parents. Mom and Dad, I'd like you to meet Moe. Unlike you murdering piles of shit, he cares about me unless the burden of loving the child of a couple who slaughtered his people is too much for him or whatever genes you animals gave me start to kick in."

She looked at Moe, tears streaming down over her cheeks.

"Please don't hate me, Moe." She looked around the room and screamed, "Please don't hate me. I was a child!"

They sat there for a while without saying anything. Moe couldn't take his eyes off the page except to look around the room.

"Someone is listening to this?" Moe asked.

"Who knows? They've been after me my whole life. Now they've found me."

"So have I," said Moe taking her hands in his. A few moments passed.

"Dear Moe, do you believe that an apple doesn't fall far from the tree?"

He looked at her. "Dear Anna, what if the tree is on a hill?"

***

From the street and boardwalk, the bungalow closest to the beach on 29th Street looked as empty and forlorn as all the Rockaway bungalows waiting for families from the city to give them a pulse and make them come alive again when school in the city was over and the human tsunami began. The rear bedroom was neither empty nor forlorn. It had had guests for months. The almost invisible two men came and went after nightfall and never left the room except to leave the bungalow. In the room were one oak table covered with empty food wrappers and an empty pizza box, a desk lamp, recording equipment, wires and cables here and there, two oak chairs and one pair of shared earphones. Until Moe discovered Anna in his kitchen, they were bored into numbness. All they had on tape was classical music and brief conversations that weren't relevant. The only usable information they gleaned in the two months was that onions should be sautéed a bit before using them in omelets to remove the water that would compromise and dilute the taste of all of the other ingredients the eggs were bombarded with. With the tape running, both men rose after Moe and Anna stopped talking and left the kitchen.

"She knows nothing," said one man to the other.

"What if she's lying to him?" the other reacted.

"What if the earth is square, putz?" reacted the other.

CHAPTER 57

The old man sat at the kitchen table finishing his third egg salad sandwich wearing a dishcloth bib for fear he would stain his new Arrow button down shirt and have to pay to have it cleaned.

Rita was in her apartment as her father and one of his foremen gathered a few pads, pencils and fifty-foot Stanley tape measures. Umberto had questioned his daughter about the proposed project, but she suggested he get his answers straight from the horse's mouth. Izolda, Priscilla and Ceci were sitting on the floor against the bedroom wall.

"He could have delusions of grandeur," said Priscilla.

"Seems pretty grounded to me," offered Ceci.

"Grounded is right. He lived in the park."

"How can a wet machine dry anything?" asked Izolda.

"Why should a man who has a few dollars live in a basement with an inside outhouse?" pondered Priscilla.

"It's better than sleeping in the park?" said Izolda.

"Something's doing with him," said Ceci, "Something's making him punish himself."

"As long as he doesn't punish us," said Priscilla.

"I guess we'll find that out sooner than later unless Izolda has more egg salad in her frig."

CHAPTER 58

The jeweler was straightening out some jewelry in the window. He saw Diego standing there holding the pizza box but disregarded him. Diego rapped his keys on the window. The jeweler gestured he should go away. Diego went to the door, balanced the pizza box in one hand and started to press the buzzer. After ceaseless buzzing, the man came to the window and yelled, "I'm going to call the police."

Diego was quick to react. "Good, you do that. But if you do, the world will know what you and your alien buddies are up to."

"You are playing with fire, young man," the jeweler cautioned.

"And you're standing next to me covered in gasoline, jefe. Listen, I'm all for the Nazis being caught and punished, but if you don't talk to me, all bets are off. I don't care what happens to me or this kosher pizza that cost me twenty bucks including the cab."

The jeweler buzzed him in, flipped the door sign to *CLOSED* and dropped the window blinds. Diego placed the pizza on the counter.

"It was you wasn't it?" asked Diego.

No reaction.

"Answer me! You're the one who started this."

"The Nazis started this."

"It was the cameo, wasn't it?

"First of all, it's a brooch; a brooch that came with her from South America, a Nazi haven. There was Yiddish on the back, and she spoke German. It doesn't belong to her or her family. It belongs to what's left of us."

"Christ!" reacted Diego. "Maybe she doesn't know about her parents."

"She does."

"How do you know?"

"We know."

"When did she know?"

"What does that matter?"

"Did she help them escape?"

"She was six. Now go."

Diego grabbed him by the shirt collar, pulled him toward the back through the stockroom door and pushed him against the wall. "Listen to me, amigo, if your buddies do anything to her or the Nazis hurt her or she's hurt in any way, I'll blow your cover. I swear I'll blow your cover and theirs."

"Look, relax, just be alert and be careful," the jeweler choked out. "We have no reason to harm her. Neither do the animals. Now let go of me."

CHAPTER 59

The old man returned to Izolda's apartment holding a shopping bag. He placed it next to his chair and sat at the kitchen table. Izolda said she had errands to run and left. Several minutes later, Umberto Ruiz walked in, introduced himself and sat opposite him.

"And your name?" asked Umberto. "I'm sure you don't want me to call you 'old man,' like they do."

As the old man extended his hand he said, "Old man is fine. Let's get started."

"You should know," said Umberto. "I'm doing this for my daughter. She's still mad at me for taking her from her school mates and friends to a place that wants nothing to do with her. But here in this situation she's alive and we get along again. Rita has invested much of herself to help you and everyone else involved. So, because of my daughter and the new peace between us, the busiest construction man in the city is taking the time to hear why more time should be taken from his family."

"She's a good girl," said the old man," and you should be proud of her. I will tell you my idea, and you will tell me if the city will approve everything, and if they do what it will cost."

"Who's paying for this?" asked Umberto.

"What does that matter as long as you're paid?"

"I know that the super's wife and the owner have no money. I also know that you sometimes live in the park and when you don't, you live in a box in the basement without a toilet. How you live is none of my business, but someone has to prove they have the ability to pay for permits, materials and labor," insisted Umberto.

"First, Mr. Ruiz, I need your word you won't discuss what we arrange with anyone including your daughter and wife. If you do, I will leave, the building will be sold for less than its value and your peace will be temporary. Umberto Ruiz nodded his approval. The old man put the shopping bag on the table in front Umberto.

"Look inside," the old man suggested.

He looked into the bag and up again.

"There's $20,000 in there," said the old man. You can take it all so you know I'm serious. If the city makes it impossible, you'll give me back ten thousand, and we'll be even. If you can do the job, I will pay you cash in advance for each part of it. I do not have a checking account, but I will open one if that's what you prefer. It's up to you."

"We can't work during the day. Uh, Mr..."

"My name is Aaron Luckman."

"Mr. Luckman, if we do this it will be during nights and weekends unless I bring in some others not in my crews. And, if I do that, only checks will do."

"If everything is approved, I'll get a checking account," said the old man.

"Okay, tell me what you want to do."

"I want to put a washer dryer in every apartment."

"You are kidding me."

"I forgot how to 'kid.'"

"Mr. Luckman, I don't have to check it out to know that your drain and electrical capacity are too low and venting could be a project killer."

"The machine washes and dries and it doesn't need a vent." said the old man.

"Washes and dries and no vents?" Rita's father reacted. "What will they think of next?"

Umberto Ruiz thought a moment before continuing.

"Mr. Luckman, there are seventy units in this building. If the city approves this thing, the cost could be prohibitive, and if they do approve, it could take at least a year."

"Then you'll have to hire extra crews," reacted the old man.

Without blinking an eye, Aaron rose and waved that he follow him into the hallway. A few feet from the opening to the kitchen, was a small alcove on the other side of the kitchen wall that had the countertop, sink and plumbing against it on the other side.

"The space is there in the same place in all of the apartments. Many tenants keep an ironing board, mops and brooms in it and hang a curtain from a tension rod to hide them. The space is big enough for a vent-less Bendix combination washer/dryer with louvre doors hiding it and their brooms and mops. My first question is can you put a drain down the outside of the building?"

"The answer is yes as long as it's vented at the top eighteen inches above the roof, has a pea trap in the wall behind the machine and a graded line one quarter inch per foot from the machine to the exterior drain. You cannot have exterior drains running down the front of the building. It'll look like a factory. So I have to see where the main city drains are and how the building drains intersect."

"Mr. Ruiz, does this mean there's a chance we wouldn't have to change the drains that are there now?"

"It means we would only connect existing plumbing for hot and cold and the existing drains would be left alone."

"This is wonderful news," reacted the old man.

"Don't celebrate yet. I have to check the diameter of the plumbing to your sinks."

He left, walked into the kitchen, opened the base cabinet doors under the sink, kneeled for a few seconds, rose and returned.

"The present plumbing would not have to change to meet code."

"That's good," reacted Aaron.

"However," Umberto continued, "a tenant will not be able to use sinks, showers and baths when the washer is in use."

"So it would be a short vacation from the sink and dishes and pots and pans," the old man reacted.

"Glass half full, I guess," smiled Umberto. "I guess our daughter was wrong."

"About what?"

"Leave me and my guys to figure this out. I'll need a few days to double check the city and try to come up with an estimate. Do both parts of the building have elevators?"

"Yes."

"Are all apartment layouts exactly the same?"

"The common hallways are a bit different, but the apartments are exactly the same. There are one-, two- and three-bedroom apartments, but the hallway and alcove are exactly the same and in the same spot in every one."

"You realize that no building owner in his right mind would do this thing."

"Yes they would if they were depending on the rents, losing tenants to new buildings, five lives depended on it, and although the person who pays for it all who expects a very fair deal, couldn't care less about money."

"That says it all, Mr. Luckman. I'll double check the building codes and get back to you after I inspect several apartments and I can take a look at all the existing plans. Please alert the tenants."

Umberto Ruiz and his team started to leave.

"Wrong about what?" asked the old man.

"What?"

"What was your daughter wrong about?"

"Oh, it's nothing," he answered.

"Let me decide."

"She said you could be impossible and that you were a negative recluse who was hiding something."

"And?"

"And nothing," he responded. "Any person my daughter cares about so much has to be pretty special. Mr. Luckman, what was your work here?"

"I removed staples from stretched and dried fur pelts."

"I know there's business in your background. What did you do in the old country?"

My father and his father were in the jewelry business."

"And what did you do?"

"I did everything...but not enough."

CHAPTER 60

Change of season at the beach was subtle at the start. As usual, the new warmth deposited during days by the higher sun was drawn back up into the evening air and made temperatures under the moonlight comfortable again. More people appeared on the boardwalk, especially seniors from the retirement homes scattered along the street side of the boardwalk from Beach Thirtieth Street in Far Rockaway to Rockaway Park a hundred streets away. Coats, scarves, knit caps and wool blankets were put away for winter's next onslaught that seemed a light year away. Finally, and once again, light sweaters would suffice. It all felt so predictable, dependable. Vendors were removing the four by eights that boarded up their storefronts. Spaces were cleaned and freshened. Facades were sanded and painted. Vending machines, amusement and kitchen contraptions were serviced and readied, and inventory was checked. It was frenetic preseason activity as usual. Eager vendors again focused on the escape from the city and joining the other entrepreneurs yearning for the vital added income, the cash portion of which would mostly evade Uncle Sam's claws. It was all about renewal and owning something.

At Moe's Bagels, life was no longer uncomplicated and predictable. There were no conversations, jokes, barbs, or opinions. Diego and Anna did their chores. Moe continued to train Diego to slice lox as uniformly as he did. He taught him how much fat he should trim and how to slice the smoked salmon into delectable, translucent slices. Diego was quiet, almost withdrawn, behavior as alien to him as snow in August.

What would be so terrible if I told them everything? he asked himself. *Maybe the spooks were listening to Anna finally telling Moe her story. Why did she open to him and not me? They couldn't have heard Anna talking to her mother and father because they would have descended on all of them by now. Could those spooks have recruited Moe to do the same thing that he was doing?*

Diego's conclusion was that they were listening to Anna confessing to Moe. The question was when did Anna discover her parents were murderers, and is she just as innocent now as she was when she was six?

He concluded, *If they're not telling me everything, why should I tell them anything?*

CHAPTER 61

The tenants were excited but didn't know exactly why. Not one of them knew what was going on, but the sign in each elevator made it insane to make a move until they knew what their landlord was talking about. Mr. Nowicki could no longer deliver the first of the "loads" of tenants he promised; a shaky start for the new bottom-line driven owner's ethically challenged superintendent. The bleeding never started. Ceci's sign froze all tenants in place. Tenants in the neighborhood actually came over to see the sign. A few took Polaroids.

DEAR TENANTS

BECAUSE OF YOUR LOYALTY, TIMELY PAYMENT OF RENTS AND YOUR TREATING THE BUILDING AS IF IT WERE YOURS, WE ARE CONTEMPLATING AN IMPROVEMENT THAT WILL MAKE YOUR APARTMENT FEEL LIKE YOUR OWN HOME. IF WE CAN DO THIS, THERE WILL BE NO INCREASE OF RENT AND ALL YOUR NEIGHBORHOOD FRIENDS WILL BE JEALOUS.

"What's happening in the building?" Mr. Nowicki asked his wife when he bumped into her in the market.

"The owner tells me nothing." she lied. "I don't even know if she'll keep me there."

She continued to walk up the aisle away from the despicable man who inadvertently helped her to become an independent woman, the bane of his fragile manhood and away from a relationship that served as the most important lesson of her young life.

"I've become such a good liar," she giggled to herself, continuing down the aisle. She felt so good, so complete.

CHAPTER 62

Almost a month had passed. They sat in the living room of Izolda's apartment waiting for Umberto Ruiz to finish his second helping of his wife's magical sopa de pollo on the floor above.

"We seem to be always waiting for someone to finish eating," Priscilla Cates murmured nervously under her breath.

"Patience partner," Ceci murmured back.

The old man hadn't said much during the month of waiting. He simply had returned to his recluse existence spending most of his time on his new bed. Now he just sat there with them. Priscilla and Ceci shared a Naugahyde rocker chair trying to rock away their nerves. Izolda and Rita sat on the carpet against the chair, their torsos moving back and forth as they all rocked in unison.

Umberto Ruiz entered the apartment. The ladies stopped rocking. He sat on the carpet his back against the opposite wall. Rita and Izolda grasped hands.

"Mr. Ruiz, I live like I do because I've had enough drama in my life," said the old man. "I want to do this and return to the life I want. Can you or can't you?"

"Old man," began Mr. Ruiz, "when I tore my family away from the life they wanted and dragged them away to the life we deserved, I told them we are all pioneers. But you, Mr. Luckman are the real pioneer. You are wasting your gift and—"

"And please get to the point," the old man interrupted.

"Permit applications and plans were approved yesterday. We can get started in a week," Umberto smiled. "Please prepare the tenants and God help us."

"What will it cost?" asked Priscilla.

"That's between that gentleman and me," he said pointing to the old man."

All eyes were on Aaron Luckman.

He turned toward Izolda, "I need a sharp scissor or something to open a seam and some dark brown thread and a needle. I have to fix my vest."

"I have a seam ripper. I'll do it for you," offered Izolda.

"No thank you," he responded.

***

The next day, the old man returned the seam ripper, needle and thread to Izolda and headed downtown carrying his valise. He walked into the Diamond Exchange on Fifth Avenue and asked for the manager and a private room. Two hours later he sat opposite the manager of The Irving Trust across from the Seagram Building on Park Avenue.

At first, the manager said that no safety deposit boxes were available and when they were, there was a waiting list and they were always in short supply. The old man put the valise on the manager's desk and lifted the lid a bit.

"Short supply?" the old man repeated. "So is a new customer who might do more than ask you to cash a paycheck every week."

He then slid the check from the Diamond Exchange across the desk. The manager asked permission to take the check and make a call. He returned, smiling, a few minutes later.

"Are you sure you don't want to put the proceeds of this check in an interest bearing account?

"Yes."

"May I ask why you chose our bank?"

"When I grew up, my best friend's name was Irving."

***

The old man was given the largest of the three sizes of boxes. In his was the product of the cashed check, the cash from the valise, and a small chamois bag with the former contents of the vest's hem. His new check book had enough in it for an advance for the job, $5000 for Umberto and another $5000 as a down payment on Umberto's daughter's education or whatever she needed. The rest of the cash and the chamois bag lay there smiling in his new safety deposit box.

***

In a brief meeting with Umberto and Ceci, he handed them signature cards so they could sign checks.

"Well do the bookkeeping here, won't we Ceci? And, Mr Ruiz, now you can go out and get all the people you need to finish the work as soon as possible."

"I'll bring in good crews I've use on other jobs. We might have it done in two months."

Umberto asked Ceci if he could have a private moment with the old man. She smiled and left.

"I want you to give Rita the gift, Mr. Luckman," said Umberto.

The old man was quick to shake his head.

"If she asks where it came from I won't lie to her."

"Then consider your bonus ten thousand and use half of it for her education," he responded. "Now there's no lie."

Umberto Ruiz put his hand on the old man's shoulders. "You're a good man with a good heart, but I can see a rope around it. I'll do what you want, but you must promise me that you'll let my daughter in. You must promise me that you'll tell her who you are, what has robbed you of life and holds you prisoner. You must tell her what drove a terrific guy like you into the bushes of Van Cortlandt Park. Both her grandparents have passed and she needs and loves you."

CHAPTER 63

Diego had arranged the meeting. The smooth crème brûlée crust that forms when the warmth of the morning sun meets the cool, dew-covered sand under the boardwalk was no longer pristine. Diego and Anna had come to the spot from different directions, fifteen minutes apart. Moe, supposedly off to Brooklyn to negotiate the season's smoked fish prices, approached them a few minutes later. The Stancatis had agreed to watch the shop for a few hours. They stood there barely after nine in the morning, and they were alone.

"It's important that each of us tell the truth to one another regardless of what happens. We have to trust each other to get through this thing," cautioned Diego.

"What thing?" asked Moe.

"Moe, with the exception of my parents, you've been the most important person in my life. You've taught me to be honest and work hard." He turned toward Anna.

"You're going to hate me, but I can never hate you regardless of what you've done or who you are. I don't care about the past. You're a beautiful person and I've let you both down."

"What the hell are you talking about?" asked Moe.

Diego told them about the encounter in the shop, the key, what the Nazi hunters did while the three of them frolicked in New York and that he agreed to keep them informed.

Anna took a deep breath. Moe put his arm around her.

"Go ahead. Let it out."

"It's out," she reacted. "It's been leaking out for years. I'm on empty. Diego, it's okay. I thought they were dead. They might as well be. I have no feelings for them as a mother and father, and I hate them as human beings. Other than that, I feel nothing."

"What can I do to make things right?" pleaded Diego.

"You can listen," she said.

After she repeated her story, Diego wiped away his tears then asked if she had the same conversation in Moe's house. She nodded yes.

"They bugged the house," he said. "They heard everything because of me."

"My house is bugged?" Moe asked, impressed.

Diego continued, "Maybe it was a good thing. Maybe it filled in the gaps. Maybe they'll leave you alone and just kill me for disobeying."

"They don't even kill Nazis," said Moe. "I think they just want them to stand in front of a judge and the world like Eichmann. Anyhow, if they hurt one of us the others will make them visible. They can't afford to be visible...Really, my house is bugged?" he asked again, proudly.

Diego nodded.

Moe raised his eyes and shook his head.

"How do you like that?"

He put his hands on Diego's shoulders.

"They must have scared you to death, but they will do nothing to you even if they know you blabbed. They're not the police, and you don't work for them. I don't like that you gave them my key, but they got what they wanted, and I still have Sylvia's silverware. Let them listen all they want. We all have nothing to hide anymore. He put his arm around both and turned them toward him.

"We all have nothing to hide, do we?"

Anna shook her head no.

"A new beginning, Anna," said Moe. "No more running. No more ghosts. No more monsters. No more nightmares. Your parents are what they are, and you are what you are. We can do what they ask of us or do nothing. What we do from now on is up to you, Anna."

"I want to see the Nazis face to face," she said. "I want to know what they want from me. I want the spies to tell me what I can do to get them hung in Israel and out of my life. I'm through running."

"How do we do this?" asked Moe.

"I have their number," said Diego.

"Let me have it, please," said Anna.

Diego took out his wallet, removed the note handed it to her. "We're going to the house, Moe. I want them to get the message, record it, listen to it and come running."

Ten minutes later, Moe and Diego watched as Anna picked up the wall phone in the kitchen and punched the number in.

Anna listened to the message and spoke. "This is Anna Rivera. I'm sure you're listening and recording. Record this:

Your men did a lousy job when they went through this house. They might as well have left a note. It's your fault. If my mother and father were as efficient as you, thousands would have been saved. Tell me where and when you want to talk to the three of us."

"And leave my key in the mailbox," added Moe.

Weeks passed without contact. They assumed they were being watched, as they went about their business and prepared for the summer invasion.

CHAPTER 64

The buzz turned into anticipation, anticipation to excitement, excitement into joy.

Mrs. Gold in apartment 6F was the first finished and had a parade of fellow tenants, a few at a time, who stood transfixed in front of the Bendix miracle.

"Do you know what Morris figured we'd save by not schlepping to the basement and feeding the machines?"

"Fifty dollars?" responded 2F.

"You're way off. Believe it or not, over a hundred and twenty-five. And neither of us has to be in that empty basement with all that's going on in the city… you know, neither of us is that young anymore."

"I didn't notice," reacted 3D.

"Morris also said using the machines in the basement had been like playing the slots in Las Vegas and winning what you already owned. When are they doing you?"

"They said maybe in a week," she answered smiling from ear to ear.

The dried wash stopped tumbling. Mrs. Gold opened the door, grabbed a piece of laundry and extended it to her. "Here, smell this."

She buried her nose in the laundry and aah'd. "Smells like perfume."

***

Barely two months had squeezed by. Far from complicated, it was a humongous cookie cutter job. Do one apartment, learn what little there was to learn, and duplicate it sixty-nine times. There were few surprises, no weakened lumber, no mold, no cockroaches or termites, no drilling or sawing through wiring. Some concrete had to be raised, dirt dug up, and more conduits joined with the main drain to the street. Additional 110 and 240 volt capacities were added. Only some painting and spackling was left to be done in a few apartments to finish the incredible installation.

Rita had watched her papa work for the first time. She had always adored and respected him. Now she was in awe of him.

She had learned about attitude and what Ceci had meant when she said, "Concentrate on solutions not problems."

Rita started doing her homework late at night. Afternoon homework time was usurped by observation and study at the graduate school of planning, leadership and control. While her schoolmates were talking about crushes and boys, cigarettes, hickies and sex, she was doing graduate work in a world that would be hers for the taking if she learned her lessons well and used them.

"Papa, I want to do what you do," she said.

"Do you?"

"Yes, very much."

"If I support your ambition will you stop complaining about the fools surrounding us and concentrate on yourself?"

"I promise."

"You have a deal."

She hugged him and wouldn't let go.

"I was the foreman on the rebuild of School of Architecture at City College," her Papa said. "They owe me. I'd rather you work with your mind, not back…and you still might have the opportunity to drive me crazy. You'd make me very proud, and you could easily fall back into construction if you prefer callouses."

CHAPTER 65

The washer/dryers had been purchased and warehoused after a price was agreed upon. It was how the old man went about disassembling the sales manager by getting an answer and commitment after each request that wowed Priscilla and Ceci.

"How much does a machine cost?" asked the old man. "How much would the discount be for five? For ten? What would it be worth to you if you could advertise that an entire apartment building was willing to invest tens of thousands just to have this miracle in every apartment? Would you consider giving some machines to us at cost if we allowed you to use our building in advertising? Would you give us a dozen as a gift?"

The manager, his shirt soaking wet, felt relieved when it was over. He sat at his desk not knowing how he should feel about the biggest sale in the chain's history. He did feel some relief that he didn't owe the old man money when the nightmare was over.

***

By the end of June, Priscilla Cates's building was like none other in New York. The building superintendents were also unique. Cecilia Papoulloute and Izolda Nowicki shared the duties of managing and servicing a building with no vacancies and a waiting list chomping at the bit.

CHAPTER 66

zolda Nowicki was in heaven. Her husband had been fired by the thirty-nine year-old general /partner/owner who had decided and convinced the tenants that there was no need for an onsite building superintendent because the management company was as good as it gets.

The old man repeated his walk in Manhattan several times a month and continued to buy a hot dog for the homeless lady in front of the delicatessen. Her name was Joanne. He looked forward to her joke every visit.

"A horse walks into a pub," she began. "He sits at the bar and asks for a seven and seven. The bartender brings her the drink and asks, "Why the long face?"

That was the last joke she told him. She wasn't there on his last visit. Concerned, the old man inquired about her. The counterman told him that they found her sitting there, dead when they opened up two weeks ago. They thought she was sleeping.

"You know she had an MBA from City College Bernard Baruch School of Business downtown," the counterman told him shaking his head. "Joanne did the store's books and taxes before she heard the voices. What a waste. The whole thing taught me a lesson. Everything is okay until it isn't. You have to make every day count."

CHAPTER 67

A few days later, Priscilla was sitting on a bench her back to the park. The old man walked by her. She beckoned he sit next to her.

"No temptation to live in the bushes anymore?" she asked.

"You've spoiled me."

"You know what kind of man my father was?"

"Rita tells me everything whether I want to hear about it or not."

Priscilla continued. "If you were homeless, sitting on this bench in rags, a dollar bill a few inches from your shoeless feet and my father passed by, he would pocket it convinced you had seen it and didn't need it."

"And you?" the old man asked. "What would you have done?"

"I probably wouldn't have noticed the bill. Maybe I wouldn't even have noticed the homeless guy."

"How come you noticed me?" asked the old man.

"I 'noticed' you?"

"Yes. You noticed me before my idea."

She continued after a moment. "So much has happened… Up until these last few months everything I've ever had was given to me. I didn't have to earn anything until lately."

"What have you earned?"

"The respect of someone I think I'm in love with."

"Your partner?"

She nodded, yes.

"Does she know how you feel?"

"I'm not sure…Ceci came such a long way after losing everything including her mother, father, sister and family business. One day she had it all and the next day she had nothing. She's so special."

"What about you?" he countered. "You had worse than nothing. At least she had everything until she had nothing. You never had anything except a roof over your head and a father who taught you nothing except how to not care, how to be unhappy, take advantage of people, how to be insecure…. and then he left you in debt. Now look at you."

"What do you see when you look at me?" she asked.

"I see someone whose life hasn't started yet; someone who must learn what makes her really happy and has to find out her true worth and how she can benefit humanity."

"Benefit humanity?"

"Why should you have to drag the anchor the past created into your future?"

"What are you suggesting?" she asked.

"I suggest that you drive me to your bank."

"I won't take another nickel from you," she asserted.

"I have no family, no rent, no bills, and no use for money. Before now I wanted to die alone. Dying is still the only thing I look forward to, but now I'm not sure I want to be alone on the way there. I expect you ladies to help me when I can't help myself…I don't want to die in a hospital or one of those places with people staring at nothing in the lobby. It's just business. I didn't want to live in the park again so I fixed that. You've already taken more than a nickel and guaranteed me a place to live and die in return. You took my money to remodel a building. Since when is a building more important than a human? I want to help you remodel yourself. It's just business."

"I don't know—"

"Yes you do. I don't think you want to live out there at the end of the earth with the ghost of your father."

"Why would you do this? What about you?" Priscilla asked. "What about your family?"

"I've checked out what mansions on the beach rent for in your neighborhood. We could fix your home up and rent it for twenty-thousand a month. If you won't take a gift, consider it a loan. You'd rather owe me money than the bank. Pay me back my monthly rental until I'm gone. It would be like an annuity for me. If God punishes me with a long life I could have a nice profit." He rose from the bench. "It's getting cold."

"Don't go," Priscilla pleaded.

"I don't want to catch pneumonia and become a burden too soon," he said as he started to leave. "Put the total amount of debt on a piece of paper, and we'll go to the bank together."

He continued to walk away.

Priscilla Cates called out to his back. "Sooner or later you're going to have to explain why you think you're worthless, old man, why you have nothing to live for… And you do have a family. I'm part of it."

CHAPTER 68

Moe, Anna and Diego sat at his kitchen table and listened to the recorded message:

You are probably being watched. This is why we do not want to pick you up. Respectfully, we'd like the three of you to meet with us in the doctors' parking lot at the Long Beach Memorial Hospital this Thursday at 9 p.m. Ms. Rivera, please go shopping in Atlantic Beach first before walking to the hospital. The other two gentlemen should come to Long Beach to dine before coming to us. Please make sure you're not being followed. We will have eyes on you just in case. Ms. Rivera and gentlemen, you are not in harm's way from our side. Decades of work have led up to this meeting. Your questions will be answered. We expect you to be there. Thank you for your patience.

"From our side?" blurted Diego. "There are sides? What do they want from us? What the hell do they want from a nineteen year-old Puerto Rican college student?"

"The same thing they want from a 65 year-old Jewish bagel maker," answered Moe. "They want our help."

"If you had let me go none of this would be happening," said Anna to Moe.

"And you would have turned around the minute your face got wet," reacted Moe, "and spent the rest of your life on your back until makeup didn't do the job anymore."

Moe took Anna by her hands.

"Dear Anna, everything is going to change. Your past, the surprises, the shocks and disappointments: They're all going to disappear the way the specials do on our blackboard when you use the damp eraser."

CHAPTER 69

The old man stayed in his apartment most of the time, but everything had changed. He no longer felt that he was alone on an island he had dredged up in some dark place in the middle of nowhere. The ladies had furnished his apartment with a few pieces of furniture and a twenty-inch RCA television set they picked up at a Salvation Army outlet. Ceci put up an aerial on the roof and dropped the aerial wire down the side of the building and connected it to the set. She rarely had to call in outside help to fix the basic plumbing and electrical problems. Much of her time was spent taking out library books that had all the answers and unclogging toilets and sinks for which the tenants had no answers.

The old man's queen-size bed was almost twice the size of the cot he had slept on for decades. A pillow top mattress made him feel he was lying on a cloud. His apartment was filled with the sound of music or news all the time. It was also filled with sunlight a few hours a day. At first he avoided it. Then Rita shouldered his upholstered chair out of the shadows across the room, faced it toward the window and made him promise he would sit in it and get some sun every day. She visited him almost every day with or without her homework. She coaxed him to the park and brought two baseball gloves and a baseball. The first time she lobbed it to him, it hit him in the chest and the experiment was over. He started to cook a little like he did a million years ago. Doing laundry in his own washer dryer was a treat. Once a week he went to Alexanders, sat on the edge of the same planter, invisible, and observed the rest of humanity while not being bothered. He looked out the bus window for the homeless man who beckoned he join him in oblivion, but he was gone. On one of those visits to the department store he noticed a Viyella blackwatch plaid shirt on a mannequin in a store window. As he stared at it he heard his father's voice:

Boychik, Scotland isn't only famous for its scotch. Come feel my Viyella shirt. It's as smooth and soft as it was twenty years ago when your mother bought it for me. Only your mother's skin is softer.

One day a young girl, pins clenched between her lips, a fresh striped button down shirt in hand, stepped into the window space and started to take the shirt off the mannequin. He rushed into the store and bought it. It fit him like a coat. He also picked up a few extra undershorts, tee shirts and a pair of argyle hose. His wardrobe now had two articles of clothing with a pattern.

Scuttlebutt suggested that the washer/dryers were his idea, and there were unsubstantiated rumors that it was his money that funded the project. He returned smiles with a nod. He found delights at his front door almost every day. His favorite was cabbage soup. Within a few months, he had tasted more than twenty interpretations of the dish.

The anti-social recluse who had used his imagination, who arranged and paid for everything, saved the building, the owners, Izolda, made seventy tenants feel they really had a home and filled a void for an aching young Puerto Rican girl, considered sharing his nightmare and pain for a fleeting second or two. He would climb out of despair from time to time and balance on the rim a bit before plunging back in.

CHAPTER 70

All Ceci's attempts to locate her family had failed. She prayed daily that they had passed quickly and without pain. Every morning while still in bed, she gazed at the few family photographs that had made the journey with her. No more tears, only smiles and gratitude she had been blessed with them. She built a stock room exactly where the old man's cube was. It was filled with piece goods and finished and unfinished karabellas. When the light was turned on it would become the most colorful eight by eight space on the planet.

Ceci was busy with the building and enjoying every minute of it. Izolda was a whiz with the used Singer sewing machine the old man had bargained for in the indoor section of the flea market on Columbus Avenue in Manhattan. When Ceci could glean an hour or two she taught Izolda how to sew the karabellas together from cut pattern pieces she brought from Haiti. The weekly call to Port-au-Prince to set things up bore results immediately. There were no jobs to be had on the island so the old employees continued to work after Ceci had left. They shared whatever money came in. There were piles of fabric and endless spools of colored thread. The tariffs on unassembled goods were very low and everyone involved stood to benefit if the girl who grew up under their noses knew what she was doing. The Haitian pattern makers, drapers and cutters who had worked for the family for decades, were prepared to cut and ship the pieces that would be sewn into the skirts and blouses in the Bronx. There were plenty of parts for machines and vats of oil to lubricate them. For now, there was no need for Ceci to pay for anything except shipping. Manufacturing labor in Haiti would be paid on the come until there was cash flow. The sewers were paid by the piece. They didn't complain about waiting a few days for the windfall they never expected before this black Haitian and her karabellas entered their lives. Most of the husbands were thrilled about the potential extra income and the relief it would provide.

The plan was that Izolda and Priscilla would man the booth and sell the karabellas at the Columbus Avenue flea market in Manhattan for a few weeks. If the results justified Ceci's excitement, Priscilla would hire, teach, supply and supervise the part timers who would man other flea markets. When justified, Izolda would find, hire and supervise tenants in the area who needed the extra income. They would set up at as many flea markets in the Metropolitan New York, Southern Connecticut and Eastern New Jersey area as they could control. It seemed as if there was an endless supply of everything needed to create something spectacular; that is if enough people wanted what they were selling.

Not only was the queue for an apartment off the charts, there was a deluge of requests for karabella sewing lessons before one piece was sold.

The old man warned Ceci that she shouldn't let her enthusiasm, the endless supply of sewers and piece goods and all the new income, if any, rush her decisions about patterns and quality. He counselled her constantly: "Measure a thousand times for you can only cut once. Overpay your help a little like Mr. Ruiz does," he added. "It's much cheaper than training new people all the time, and don't over-promise your help or customers. Employees give more and customers pay more for the truth. However, the most important piece of advice he imparted was: "Don't hire anyone unless you're convinced he or she needs the job, can be trusted with cash and most important, you would be happy, secure and content if everyone who worked for you was exactly like him or her."

As for the partnership of Priscilla Cates and Cecilia Papalouloute, it was perfect. Each lady had 50 percent regardless of who did what or when or the amount of money an individual effort produced. Both felt money was not a goal; instead, it was only a byproduct of something far more important.

Priscilla, Izolda and Ceci were together for the first Sunday at the flea market. The team, their sales ability less than honed, sold out the first twenty pieces in an hour and a half and took orders for twenty more before they wrapped up. Priscilla observed it all in awe and was ecstatic. Although she first doubted her partner's venture would provide them with enough extra cash to buy bicycles, today she had watched a fortune literally manufactured from whole cloth. As they packed up, Priscilla looked up and saw Ceci gazing at her.

CHAPTER 71

Priscilla had soloed back and forth to the Hamptons several times to check out the house. Without Ceci there, visiting her birthplace was an obligation not a homecoming. The old man's offer poured into the emptiness each time she left her future in the cramped but energized apartment and headed toward the empty beach mansion, isolation and her depressing past.

"Murray Cates should see his daughter now," she thought to herself, "sharing an apartment in a building surrounded by brick and layers of 'those' people, rubbing elbows with a Puerto Rican, a Pole and a Black, sleeping on a cot mattress as thick as one of his cigars."

On the next trip to the house, eager to continue her giant leap to self-sufficiency, she grabbed her father's heavy surf rod and box of lures and drove to Montauk, the northeastern tip of Long Island. She had checked into Gurney's Inn, gobbled down two lobster rolls and struggled to digest them until she left for the beach. It was four AM, and it was cold. Surrounded by pickups, headlights beaming into the Atlantic, she made her first cast with no Murray Cates by her side. The lure was snapped up the moment it hit the water. A chilling, epithet-inundated hour later, after having walked under or around dozens of fishing lines, through countless headlight beams, she landed the humongous, exhausted striper over a mile south of the cast. Priscilla Cates, self-sufficient single woman, now suffering from sinusitis, dragged it in shallow water back to where it all started. She bagged it and brought it to the supermarket where they cleaned, boned, filleted it and placed it on the ice in the picnic cooler she was forced to buy. Almost home with her catch, she drove by Mr. Peterson, his key in the bank's front door and made a decision. She screeched an illegal U-turn and pulled up opposite him. Peterson heard the tires and recognized the car. He walked over.

"Good morning, Ms. Cates. All that rubber for me?" Peterson smiled.

"Please have my balance on the home equity loan and the mortgage including back taxes by tomorrow morning. I'll be calling you first thing," said Priscilla disregarding his question. She then made another u-turn and headed home.

During the next month or so the house and taxes were paid off, repairs made, some painting done, the house scrubbed clean by some of Ceci's Haitian lady friends, some furniture updated, the rental listed, and within a few weeks a guy who owned a square block in Manhattan and an island somewhere near St. Thomas handed Priscilla a check for thirty thousand dollars to cover the security and first month's rent. She couldn't stop vibrating on the way back to Riverdale and her cot.

In four months, the old man would have his investment back, and she would continue to explore her potential.

CHAPTER 72

There were only a few cars in the parking lot. Visiting hours were over and most doctors had already visited their hospitalized patients. Anna had arrived early and was pacing around when Moe and Diego pulled in and got out of the car. Anna joined them. A black station wagon, headlamps off, started toward them and stopped a few feet away. The passenger door opened, a man exited, opened the rear door and gestured they get in.

"Shalom," said the man who had lectured Diego at the shop. "My name is Benjamin, and his name is Joseph," he said pointing to the driver. "We're going to a place where we can talk more comfortably. Thank you for coming."

They drove east for ten minutes or so to a small beachfront house at the end of the last street in Point Lookout, Long Island.

They were all seated at a dining room table. A lantern on the center provided the only light. The shades were drawn. It looked like the preparation for a séance. Joseph spoke the first words.

"We ask ourselves, when does this all end? Who will decide when justice has run its course? Is it possible that thousands will get away with their crimes? Is it possible humanity will forget? The answer is yes, but will we ever stop? Only when the last criminal is found or dies from an accident or illness or of old age…and if any of those things happen first, we will kill his or her legacy."

Benjamin looked at Anna and asked, "By what name would you like to be called?"

"What am I guilty of?" she asked disregarding the question.

"You are guilty of nothing," answered Benjamin.

"We are convinced that you are a victim," added Joseph.

"My name is Anna."

"Why do you run, Anna?" asked Benjamin.

"Why do I run?" she reacted, annoyed. "Haven't you been listening to me? Maybe it's time you heard me in person instead of on a microphone."

"Good enough," said Joseph. "What we have to say can wait."

"And maybe it's time the two of you should know me better," she said, looking at Moe and Diego.

"My parents always treated me like an adult, but of course you have that on tape, don't you?" She stared through Joseph. "They would have told me they went to look at a winery. They would have taken me with them even in the middle of the night. If it was some sort of emergency they would have come to me and explained what was going on. Instead, they left me without saying a word, without saying goodbye."

Anna rose and started pacing around the table.

"I asked myself how they could have ever loved me," she said. "Were we a lie? Was it all just a lie? The Olafsons, or whatever the hell their real name is, also lied to me for years. I hope you did a better job finding them…There's nothing complicated or personal here, mind you. Just like my mother and father, their survival was more important than mine…So did anyone love me?"

She shrugged.

"I ended up in Buenos Aires in a place for difficult children. There, in that hell, only parts of me received their 'love.'"

Benjamin and Joseph didn't react. Tears started streaming down Moe's cheeks. Diego placed his hands over his eyes and turned away.

Anna continued, "I was angry and lost. I didn't trust anyone, and so I decided to run from everything. I made it all the way to Mexico. And then I saw my mother and father on the cover of La Prensa in Veracruz, the final proof that their survival was more important than mine. But I don't understand why you've been after me for so long."

"All we wanted was information. We thought that maybe you knew something that could be useful," said Joseph.

"And we were never after you," added Benjamin. "We were and still are after them and their network of Nazi criminals and sympathizers who escaped justice. We wanted to be there when they made contact. We know they always want to make sure that you are okay, and that is their weakness."

"How can people like them care about anyone or anything?" asked Moe.

Benjamin answered, "Hitler slaughtered millions of mothers while demonstrating his intense love for his own. I'm sure he would have had the same love for a daughter."

Joseph continued, "Anna, all they had and still have to do is run and hide, but they don't. They run, stop, observe their daughter then evaporate when we're getting close. We almost had them in Veracruz and came closer when they detoured to Mexico City. There, one of our colleagues who's head of radiology at Hospital de Jesus, alerted our group that a middle age couple that fit their description had paid cash for an exam that included full body scans. Even more unusual than a Dr. Goldberg heading a department at a Catholic hospital was that both probably had cancer. The male had a mass at his duodenum and the lady masses in her breast and femur. There were no other tests. They left us with patently false personal information and great images of the bastards on surveillance tapes. We were minutes late. The next time we were close was in Atlantic Beach. A retired colleague of ours thought he saw them running on the beach every day. He followed them in his car until they ended up on The Atlantic Beach Bridge and set up a land scope. We searched every bungalow and questioned all of the owners. In a few hours, we were looking at them on copies of their French Canadian passport pictures. We missed them by a few hours. We set up our own land scope in the same position on the bridge, and there you were, Anna, on the porch reading a magazine. Their scope was probably powerful enough to read with you."

Joseph rose and spoke. "My colleagues and I are convinced that sooner than later they will make contact with you. We know they are both sick, and time is a factor. That's why they've been so careless this time. We expect you to call us immediately if they reach out to you in any way or if you suspect they are near."

Anna sat down, thinking aloud. "I was told that I was born in Bariloche, Argentina. I never questioned that, but I have memories of being sick to my stomach for days on a ship. It was not on a lake. I've seen pictures of Gibraltar. I remember seeing the shape in my dreams.

First I ran from pain and disillusionment, then, after I saw them in their uniforms staring at me from the front page in Vera Cruz, I ran from their genes. I'm good at running. I'm not good at staying. For many moments here and there I was convinced I shouldn't stay on the planet. That's all changed now."

Joseph sat next to her. "We must tell you something, Anna."

He reached for an envelope in his briefcase, took out copies of several ledger pages, some photographs, a letter and a hospital's medical record and pushed them across the table to Anna. "Anna, I know you are fluent in German, but I will save you the time.

"Brunner and Willman met in Berlin in 1936 and married in 1939. Oberleutnant Oskar Brunner of the Einsatzgruppen looks formidable in his SS uniform doesn't he? He and his wife traveled to various cities. He instructed the local officers how to decide which Jews would be herded on to the trains to the camps and furnaces and which were taken to the woods and shot.

Joseph pointed to the other photo.

"Vera Else Willman also looks proud and formidable in her Nazi shirt, skirt, wide belt and boots. She taught the soldiers and locals how to sort the abandoned belongings of the Jews on the way to oblivion. Only Frau Goebbels, Leni Riefenstahl, Hanna Reich, and a few other women were called Reichfürerin, important women of valor in the war effort. We understood why Frau Goebbels, Riefenstahl and some others were not expected to make a home, cook for their husbands, and have Nazi babies, but we couldn't understand why the wife of a bit player was permitted to serve the Reich instead of her husband, that is until we uncovered these medical and hospital records last week. Vera Else Willman had a total hysterectomy to remove tumors on her ovaries in 1933, three years before she met her husband."

CHAPTER 73

Successful Jewish sons and black athletes have several things in common, the most palpable being a genetic disposition to buy their mothers a house as a thank you for surviving their childhood whether it was sweltering at Little League games or the principal's office. The son and daughter-in-law of the elderly couple in 6B bought a condo for them in Sunrise, Florida, a few miles from their home on the Inland Waterway in Boca Raton, a slice of kosher heaven they had relocated to two children ago. His mother and father had resisted uprooting their roots in concrete and moving to Florida long before their son had married, but their adamant stand weakened with each grandchild and evaporated when Grandpa was diagnosed with Parkinson's. And so, 6B was vacant for a few minutes.

A few years before the vacancy, Estelle Cohen, Hunter College graduate and CPA had fallen head over heels in love with Sid Lehrman and immediately put her name on the list for a two bedroom in the building just in case. It had been his cha-cha at first sight on the temporary dance floor at the Adath Israel Jewish Center in the Bronx. She loved his looks, his confidence, his fantastic mambo moves his pirouettes and while they were dancing, his diatribe about and objection to the war in Vietnam; a war he felt was unjust and unnecessary. The draft notice came two weeks before they were to be married at the same synagogue. Speeding north to Canada, she called her parents from a gas station in Buffalo, brought them up to date on their flight and promised she would come back and take both of them to their new home as soon as they were settled in Canada.

She was gobbled up by a tax preparation chain and working sixty hours a week before the stamp dried on her passport. What she discovered, to her chagrin, was that the man she thought she loved not only conscientiously objected to the war, he conscientiously objected to working. After ten months and a non-effective passionate sermon or ten she concluded that if Sid Lehrman was Mikhail Baryshnikov and sat around between performances it would be tolerable. Sidney Lehrman was no Mikhail Baryshnikov. She fled back to New York and her thrilled father just as her name reached number one on the queue for a two-bedroom.

The apartment was well-kept with a park view if the craning neck was young or was winning the battle against cervical arthritis and the attached head had eyes that had the peripheral vision of a hammerhead shark.

CHAPTER 74

Not a word was spoken on the way back to the hospital parking lot and home. The drama had ended. In its place was a void. Diego's mind was spinning as Moe's car left the parking lot. Life had been so simple: A mom and dad, pressure to be a good human being and not abandon decency for any reason. He would finish college, graduate, be his own man and make his parents proud and secure when and if they needed help; an indelible game plan.

Was this person he had befriended out of his league, too complex? Was he mature enough, worldly enough, wise enough to be her companion? What could he contribute? How could he help her? Was he trivia now? She's had several lives all of which she had to negotiate alone. Someone had held his hand since he was born. She was a woman. He was a boy.

Moe never made it into his house. He spent the night on his rocking chair on the front porch. Was she strong enough to survive it all? He tried to focus on something else, but couldn't. When he closed his eyes he saw her being violated. Then he imagined her sitting on her bed waiting for her parents to show up.

All right, he said to himself. She had her 'I've had it' moment, but would she have turned around had he not waded after her? Now she had much too much invested in surviving. There was no victim in this woman. She never hung in there, she ran and climbed. But he also knew that when you remove the foundation from a building the structure is doomed. Who would she be now, now that she bared her tragedy to all and her parents weren't her parents? And what do you talk about from this point on? The answer came quickly. Rebuild the foundation. She must find out who she is. He was shaking his head, yes, without a clue how to convince her that if she found them her story could be just beginning.

CHAPTER 75

On some not so hot days, frugal tenants didn't use their air conditioners in order to save on their utility bills. They relied on the cross-ventilation open windows and wedged-open front doors created. On some floors the rhythmic sound of sewing machines seeped into the hallway with the breeze. The new entrepreneurs were in five flea markets within forty-five minutes of Riverdale. Priscilla had elected to work the flea market in Fort Lee, a few minutes from the Jersey side of the Washington Bridge. It was only a half an hour drive from her hotel room at the Concourse Plaza hotel in The Bronx. She no longer stood like a statue until someone showed interest and came over. Priscilla continuously explored how far she could escape her imaginary boundaries. Instead of being against the display waiting for passers bye to come over, she would now stand a few feet in front of the booth wearing a karabella outfit and holding one in front of her on a hanger. A trainee would stand there and learn from this person who a few months ago sat in her front yard completely dependent on others.

"Made in America with fabric from Haiti to support starving Haitians, and these will be twice the price sooner than later. Get some spice in your life. They'll never be this price again.

Hi miss. Isn't it a great day? Come on over here and let me show you the new rage. You can try on the top over your T-shirt. I'll hold your bag."

Priscilla had turned the page. Although she would never stop loving her father, her self-respect nudged him into subtext for the rest of her life.

CHAPTER 76

June flew by. Crowds, beach chairs, sandy blankets, pails, shovels and grandmas keeping an eye on two year-olds sitting in an inch of water making sure they didn't drown had replaced the chilled, grey, baron Rockaway off-season. Anna and Diego sat on the wooden steps down to the beach staring out over the umbrellas to the sea until he broke the silence.

"Anna, do you believe in spontaneous generation?"

"Diego, not again! Enough, please! I know that a man and woman made me."

Diego persisted, "What if your parents were decent people, Anna? What if the bastards took you away from them? What if they've spent their entire lives not knowing if their daughter was dead or alive. If they're still alive, they haven't had one happy moment not knowing if, who or where you are. Anna, you will never find true happiness unless you know everything about who you are and where you came from."

"My goal is not to find happiness," she countered. "It's a fool's errand. My goal is to get through today."

"You cannot have a future without a past." Diego shot back.

"Where did you get that from?" she asked.

"I think it was a Lone Ranger thing. I think Tonto said it to him."

"Diego, what if they found me in an alley? And if we do find them, what then? They're going to want to know what their daughter has done with her life."

"I can answer them if you're afraid to," Diego jumped in. "Their marvelous daughter has survived the most awful calamities, and all the horrors she experienced haven't robbed her of her courage, her pride and beautiful heart. I don't care who or where they are, they will love and respect you. Anna, for all you know they had to survive horrors worse than yours. For all you know, they've spent their lives looking for you and never had a good day."

CHAPTER 77

Anna had been chained to a myth. Now, the myth and the chain were gone, and all but one blank was filled in. She asked for time off. Moe resisted at first trying to convince her that the best thing for her was to lose herself in her work. She couldn't. More and more of her time was spent alone sitting on the boardwalk looking out to sea. From time to time she'd place a blanket and beach chair on the sand and spend hours gazing at the eastern horizon not the book on her lap. She'd throw the book on the blanket, roll up the bottoms of her dungarees and head toward the ocean. She walked through the foam until her ankles were caressed by six inches of the Atlantic. Once again, the Gulf Stream had done its magic; the ocean was warm and smooth. She wondered when and if her personal winter would end; whether the water would ever be as warm and smooth as the night before the monsters abandoned her.

Last week, every day at sun up, while the spooks slept, she had planted herself on the beach and looked out at the horizon and her future. Each morning she watched the same two figures fishing only hundred yards from shore. She sat and watched as their small craft gently rose and fell. As far as she could tell, not one fish was pulled into the boat, and yet they remained in the same spot for a week. She finally asked herself who would be so ill-advised or stupid to not look for a more fruitful location. The answer came quickly. She slowly rose, put the book on the chair, put her sunglasses on the book, placed a terry wrap around her shoulders and slowly walked across the sand, up the stairs, across the boardwalk, and when she turned and couldn't see the ocean anymore, raced to the house and the kitchen phone. Anna turned on the recording feature of Moe's new Motorola answering machine, lifted the phone from the cradle and dialed the number on the slip of paper in her other hand. Someone picked up and said, "Yes?"

"You know who I am, Joseph."

"Yes, I do, Anna. What can I do for you?"

"I know you are recording this, and so am I. Listen closely. There's no time to repeat myself or have a conversation."

"What's going on?"

"Write this down."

"Okay."

"I'm preparing an agreement for you to sign. It says that you will make every effort to find my real mother and father and that you will spare no time or money doing so. If you don't agree, your best chance of capturing the Nazis will evaporate.

"And when do you want this agreement, boss?"

"It'll be here waiting for you. When you sign it and give me your recorded word, I'll tell you where they are."

"Are they near you now?"

"When can I expect you?"

"We're a few blocks from you."

"Then hurry."

As soon as she hung up she dialed the shop. Moe answered.

"Is Diego there?" she asked.

"Yes. Why?"

"Let him watch the place. Please get in your car and hurry home."

He was in the kitchen in less than ten minutes. The agreement was written in five. Joseph took fifteen to get there because of the need for an 'approval' call he made to headquarters in Israel.

Business completed, they hurried to the boardwalk.

Joseph told her to casually return to her chair, took out his binoculars and watched the small outboard power up, turn and disappear into the mist as it headed south along the coast. They hurried to a waiting car. Anna sat on the rear seat next to Moe who she insisted had to be with her. Joseph sat next to the driver talking a mile a minute on a crackling two way device. As they approached the humongous parking lot at Beach 29th Street, helicopter wheels touched down on the asphalt. Blades slowly rotating, the pilot beckoned they hurry and board. He positioned Anna and Moe on a ledge at the back of the cockpit and strapped them in. Joseph sat next to him. As the helicopter rose and headed west, Moe asked, "Why are you flying inland?"

"To make ourselves less obvious, answered the pilot. We'll land from the west.

Joseph added, "It's unfortunate, but we had to alert the Coast Guard, because we need the coverage. We have no assets on the ocean or along the beach between here and the Marina at Belle Harbor. The Marina is the only place they could have rented the boat. We assume they feel safe and will return it. If not, it's as you say in America, a crap-shoot."

Anna grabbed Moe's hand and gripped it until it hurt.

Evaporation from the warm sea continued to create morning mist. The mist became a thin layer of fog that would last until the sun did it in.

"Anna, you are with us as a courtesy. You will not have time to talk to them, but I promise you that if we grab them, you will before we move them out of the country."

The helicopter was in the air a mere 10 minutes before it landed on the parking lot hugging the Belle Harbor marina and beach. They headed to a small café yards away at the marina. There were now several cars parked facing the chain link, low dunes, the beach and the ocean. At the far western end of the lot, a dozen police and Coast Guard vehicles sat waiting. Visibility was less than a hundred yards or so. Anna, nervous, sat in the car gazing out at a sea, ready to confront the two imposters who had doted over her for seven years and abandoned her for twenty-five.

CHAPTER 78

The old man hadn't slept in days. He had spent the time on buses crisscrossing the Bronx and Manhattan. It was a Sunday. He had dozed a bit on the train to Manhattan and given up searching for a reason to exist. Central Park, bathed in sunshine, was humming with humanity. He wondered how Utrillo and Renoir would capture this oasis for those seeking relief from brick and concrete, seeking a change in their outlook, relief from an oppressive work week or lousy relationship. How would they paint those looking for love, others who found it, walkers and sitters, sprinters and joggers, parasols, bicycles, strollers and carriages and children being children. He wondered how their brush strokes would interpret the husbands and wives, partners and lovers experiencing the pure joy of watching their tiny creations playing with abandon and blossoming in front of their eyes.

The old man picked up a half empty Silvercup bag of sliced white bread and walked to the edge of The Central Park Reservoir better known as The Lake. The races to the floating pieces of white bread he cast were a losing proposition for the slower ducklings. He tossed the remaining chunks out as far as he could then showered the trailing ducklings with crumbs. He walked to a bench, deposited the empty bag in a refuse can then sat. At the next bench, a woman sat with her prone husband's head on her lap. Both were reading as their baby cried in their carriage. When the baby started screaming "Papa," the old man rose walked over and demanded the couple attend to their child. They both sat there shaking their heads in confusion pointing to the carriage. The old man looked inside. The baby was sleeping peacefully, but the screaming continued. He backed away, shaking, and then rushed to the 72nd Street exit.

CHAPTER 79

"He's not on the roof or in the basement or in the park," said Izolda.

"That's two days he hasn't slept in his bed," reported Rita.

"He's probably taking a break," said Ceci.

"From what?" asked Priscilla.

"From us," she answered.

"He loves us," said Rita.

"How can you tell?" asked Ceci.

"Every time I see him I think it will be the last, moaned Rita. I'm so worried."

"We have to do something," blurted Priscilla.

"Chain him to his refrigerator?" asked Ceci.

"For Christ's sake, Ceci," shouted Priscilla, "Tell me who's benefitted from having Aaron Luckman in our lives more than you have? Isn't there more to you than business?"

Ceci shot back, "I would have made it without him because I know who I am and I refuse to fail. That doesn't mean that he didn't do remarkable things for all of us but spare me, and I don't want to hear about this 'life raft' crap. Each one of us would have made it sooner or later if we wanted it badly enough and were willing to do the work."

"You're not saying a quadruple amputee could win a marathon, are you Ceci?" asked Priscilla.

"No, my facetious partner. I'm saying that finding him is not as important as helping him to face how he got this way. That's the only way he has a chance."

Heads nodded in agreement.

"So I have a question for all of you," Ceci continued. "Are you all willing to do the work?"

"Yes," they said in unison.

Rita jumped in, "This is great. It's like that old Chinese saying –

Giving a starving person some fish to eat is not as important as teaching him how to fish."

"What if he doesn't like fish?" asked Izolda.

"God help us," reacted Ceci looking up at the ceiling.

"I'll give you the Polish version, Izzie," said Rita. "Feeding him a sausage is not as important as teaching him how to catch one."

"Rita," ordered Ceci, "while Izolda's processing that, get to his room and take clearer pictures of the people in the street, the street signs and what there is of the store front you were talking about in his photographs,. If the Polaroid doesn't do the job, buy a Nikon with a close up lens, take the pictures and return it because you're not happy. I'll give you the money."

"Actually," said Rita. "That won't be a lie. I'll be unhappy I have to return it."

"I'm going to contact an immigration attorney for myself," said Ceci. "I'll find someone to help us get more information about who he is and where he came from. We must get a photo of the tattoos on his arm."

CHAPTER 80

The thick fog was translucent again. Through it came the shape of a large, black inflatable towing a fifteen foot outboard that appeared empty. As it neared, a crackling voice shouted, "We have them."

Joseph and Moe sprung out of the car. Joseph lifted his Mossad .22 out of his hip holster as they raced toward the slip the inflatable was heading for. Anna, ashen white, sat for a moment then followed. She stopped yards from the dock. The others gazed down at the nude male and female lying against each other in pooled blood on the bottom of the boat. The dead man clutched a note in his hand. Joseph jumped into the boat, looked the bodies over, took a photo of the faces of the man and woman, gently removed the note from the male's hand and climbed back on the dock. Anna was still frozen in place. Joseph walked over to her.

"Oberleutnant Oskar Brunner and Vera Elsa Willman are both dead. Looks like he shot her and then himself. They left a note for us. Do you want me to read it?"

Anna nodded.

To the Jews: You couldn't catch us, but cancer did. To Anna: You are and always will be our daughter.

Anna walked to the edge of the slip peered down at them. Moe finally took her by the waist and pulled her away.

CHAPTER 81

Rita looked up and down the block standing watch on the building's steps. No one knew when or if the old man would return. The ladies had scoured every inch of his apartment. No revelations. Rita used her new Nikon and macro-lens to reshoot the two photos they already had, the naturalization document dated 1952, proof of Aaron Luckman's U.S. citizenship in 1954 and his social security card. There were a few Staten Island Ferry ticket stubs and an expired annual pass to The Statue of Liberty. In plain sight, Berkowitz's note wrapped around 50 new one hundred dollar bills was more proof that the old man didn't care much about the present or future.

They took turns reading the Berkowitz note advising Aaron Luckman to smell the roses.

Ceci shook her head. "This Berkowitz tried, but he was giving driving lessons to a blind man."

"Feeding him advice like this can't hurt," said Izolda.

"It can't help either," countered Priscilla, "It's like counselling a man who's already swallowed the poison."

Ceci took charge. "Enough excuses. Let's first place the streets in the photos in a country, a town and a neighborhood and check if there's anything we can find out about the store. If I had to bet, I'd bet that these two (pointing at the photograph) are the grandparents with their infant grandson or granddaughter, and this is the weary mother. She's pretty. It's very possible; In fact it's likely, that the man who took the photo is their son, her husband and the baby's father. Maybe he's the old man?"

A voice came from the open doorway to the corridor.

"Hello, I'm Estelle Cohen. I rent apartment 5C. Is this a private meeting?"

"We're just checking a leak," shouted Ceci. "We'll be out in a few seconds."

They walked into the hallway and found the new tenant waiting and smiling.

And as if it were one sentence, she poured out the following without taking a breath.

"I've been here almost a month and couldn't help noticing so many tenants working from home. I guess it's none of my business, but is this some sort of cooperative? I asked my next door neighbor, Mrs. Giordano, what she was doing and she suggested I go see the booth at the Columbus Avenue flea market. I bought one outfit and my father loves me in it. He lives with me, and he makes me wear it around the apartment when it's overcast because it brightens things up. He thinks the outfit could be helpful when you're depressed. Do you have a need for an accountant? Before you answer, let me caution you that cottage industries seem to be IRS's favorite prey at the moment. I graduated from Hunter College at the head of my class and received my CPA just before my fiancée and I left for Canada."

"Slow up. After you take a breath and relax we'll continue," said Ceci.

"I'm sorry if I was a bit over the top," she apologized.

"Your father must be a nervous wreck," said Priscilla.

"I'm only this way when I'm enthused."

"Maybe you should come back when you're depressed."

"My father said that the outfit made me look—"

"Your fiancée is a draft dodger?" asked Priscilla butting in.

"Actually, my ex-fiancée is a draft dodger. I discovered he also dodges work and responsibility. Seems that the only thing he didn't dodge was the toilet rim and floor around it."

"Welcome to the Ladies without Babies Club of Riverdale." Priscilla bowed.

Ceci jumped in. "We might need someone who knows the ins and outs of employing people who work at home. And we might need another pair of eyes with a trained brain to squeeze every net nickel out of gross. Right now, I do most of the money things, but I really want to concentrate on ordering fabrics and carving out a few hours a week to concentrate on the next project I'm excited about. Eventually, we might need someone who handles the recruiting, training and supervision of our vendors if my partner decides she's bored, and I hope she gets bored sooner than later. We have other fish to fry. I'm hunting for a project that I can use our existing sewers on. I don't believe in dead ends. How does all this sound to you Estelle? May I call you Estelle?"

"Fantastic," she blurted. "You can call me anything you want."

Ceci continued, "This is an interstate business. We also sell in New Jersey and Connecticut and want to expand. It could get complicated."

"Maybe on rare occasions I might need advice," Estelle Cohen said, "but hire me and you get the retired, ultra-wise founding partner of Cohen, Clancy and Adelman, one of the oldest accounting firms in the city."

"What about pay?" asked Priscilla.

"We're financially okay for now. Listen, I'm here because I don't want to be a termite in one of the high-rise mounds downtown. I also want to spend more time with dad. How about free rent and 600 a month until I'm indispensable?"

"Priscilla looked at Ceci. "I guess my partner and I will have to discuss—"

"That was a good discussion," Ceci interrupted. "You're hired."

"One more thing," said their new employee. "I want a skyscraper not six-story career."

"I just about swam from Haiti," said Ceci, as she hugged Priscilla to her side. "My partner just threw away her crutches to shoot for the moon. As for me and these other ladies, including the girl standing outside the building, we don't hang in there. We climb."

CHAPTER 82

The old man dragged what was left of him south on the west side of Central Park West. The fleeting thoughts of renewal he sometimes felt when bathed in the warmth of the afternoon sun were gone. He gazed to the right at Lincoln Center, as he passed and realized he would never see the inside or hear its voice. If he did what he now intended to do, there would be no baroque string quartet welcoming him after the deed was done. There'd be no more memories, thoughts, challenges or observations. The last thing he would observe as guilt faded into oblivion would be the algae-covered bottoms of the pilings against a wooden quay as he descended through the flotsam into the blackness of the East River.

He kept walking until he passed the familiar Holy Trinity Lutheran Church on the corner of 65th Street and the park. Handel's *Messiah* poured out through the church's open doors and froze him. The choir was as magnificent as ever. The old man was overwhelmed by the product of Handel's belief in and love of God. He started sobbing. Passersby looked at him as they approached, looked back at him after they passed. He stopped crying, wiped his wet face with his hands, stood there for minutes staring at the pavement. A pastor, who had observed him from the doorway, descended the steps, approached and took his arm.

"Good afternoon, brother. I'm Pastor Thomas. Why are you not sitting in the last row inside as always?"

The old man kept staring at the pavement. The pastor nudged his chin up and looked into what was left of the blue in his tired eyes.

"You have that 'I've had enough' look in your eyes. Whatever you're thinking of doing can wait for a bit. Let's go inside."

He took him by the arm and they walked up the steps.

Before they entered the church the pastor continued. "You know what Beethoven said about Handel? He said, "Go to him to learn how to achieve great effects, by such simple means."

I'm sure that Handel would prefer we sit and listen to his music. And I would like very much to listen to your music as well. Even though it might be sad, maybe the two of us can a great effect."

CHAPTER 83

Anna showed up at work the next morning after Moe had insisted she take off a week or so with pay to sort out what had happened and what it meant to her. She was clearing a table when Moe walked in. He gave her a *what are you doing here?* Look.

"Moe, I'm 36, and I don't know who I am, where I came from and if my family is alive somewhere. I don't know if I have brothers or sisters, aunts and uncles, cousins. Joseph will be here when we close. I want them to find the answers to all my questions in return for what I did for the two of them, for the Jews and the rest of the world. I want to be born all over again and have a fresh start, and I want you and Diego to be in my corner until and after I have answers."

Moe looked at her, walked over, took her hands. "Of course we'll always be in your corner, but if you come up empty, I want you to believe that you have already been reborn and you have a family."

"I know, Moe, it just isn't enough. There's a black hole in my life, and I have to jump in."

"Anna, what if there's no bottom?"

"I can't spend the rest of my life living at the edge. I have to do this, and they'll have to help me after what I did for them.

CHAPTER 84

The concert was over. The buzz echoed off the vaulted ceilings and walls of the marvelous space. Thankful attendees streamed out into the late afternoon sun. Some shook the parson's hand and thanked him. It had been the last concert of the day. Church members started to clear away music stands, speakers and paraphernalia. Within a few minutes, the parson and old man were sitting alone in the last row. The parson beckoned Aaron follow him into a small chapel off the side aisle. They sat on an upholstered bench, both staring forward.

"Does your family know how unhappy you are?" asked the parson.

"I have no family."

"What about your friends and acquaintances?"

"I have four acquaintances, three women and a girl. They are concerned about me and try their best. They don't know who or why I am."

"And who are you?"

There was no response.

"Do they know why you're so depressed?"

"No."

"Do you know why you're so depressed?"

No response.

"Do they know you want to end your life?"

"I think so."

"Are you healthy?"

"I don't know."

"Aaron, why don't you want to go on living?"

"I'm not living. I exist to be punished."

"Do you believe there's a God?"

"I'm a Polish Jew who was living in Krakow in 1939. What do you think?"

"Are you a survivor?"

"I didn't survive."

The old man rose to leave. The parson tugged him down by the sleeve.

"I cannot offer you much, but if you are really headed toward oblivion, the passage will be easier if you share your burden, if you share your story with someone. You don't have to be a Christian to experience the relief of confession. Leave your sins with me if not with God."

The old man slumped and held his temples in his palms. After five minutes passed he started to talk.

"I was a good son and a good husband and father. My father's father started our business in 1877, forty years before the Russian Revolution and World War 1. My father trusted me with any negotiation including buying the precious stones our artists used in pieces we designed. My mother and wife were exquisite, beautiful inside and out. My father was stern but loving and generous. I was born in 1906. That my wife, Ruth, a 21-year-old beauty that every young man in Kazimierz wanted, chose me a plain 30 year-old, was a miracle, and that she gave us gave us Rachel a year later was another miracle.

Generations of our family, the jewelry shop, our home next to it on Szeroka Street, had survived whatever history threw at us until Hitler. Nazi officers shopped at our shop. They demanded discounts on all the jewelry they bought for their mistresses and wives, but they were stupid and overpaid for much of what they bought. They treated us like trash, like the things one discards without thinking twice. We could not imagine they planned to discard an entire people. In 1939, when the animals poured into Krakow, we talked about leaving but didn't. Some neighbors were forced to move into the countryside, many just disappeared. A few times a week you would see a Mercedes SS officer's car leading a truck. As the truck passed you would see the rolled up canvas and SS men sitting in the back facing each other like statues, rifles between their legs. If they stopped at a home or business, the occupants would never be seen again. We knew the ghetto was almost finished. I begged my father and mother to try to figure out an escape plan, but everything happened so fast. Although my parents wanted to stay, they wanted us to leave and take their hearts with us. I started to investigate some ways of leaving Krakow.

"It was January 11, 1941. I was on the way back from negotiating and buying several diamonds, some emeralds and rubies from an old vendor who had decided to unload his stock to have enough cash to pay their way out of Krakow and escape what they were convinced was our fate. There was snow on the ground and more was falling. He begged me to take my family and run. He told me how to duplicate his departure and gave me the names of officials and others who could be paid off for their cooperation and assistance to get us Swiss passports and other documents. My mother, father and I spoke enough Swiss and German to be convincing. He insisted his wife sew the jewels into the hem of my vest just in case. It all sounded quite possible, even though I knew how difficult it would be to convince my mother and father to leave everything behind except some jewels. I decided I would use our baby, the grandchild they had prayed for day and night, to convince them to leave with us.

I rehearsed what I'd say over and over again: *Your grand-daughter will need her grandmother to take care of her while the rest of us build a new business in a new country. And she'll need her grandfather's wisdom to guide her as he guided me.*"

The old man stopped talking.

"Please go on."

"I'm finished talking. Thank you," he said, as he rose.

"My name is Pastor Thomas Preston. They call me Pastor Tom. Tell me your name," he asked as he took the old man's hand.

"Aaron Luckman is the name they gave me on Ellis Island. My real name is Aaron Lukasiewicz. I use the name they gave me because I despise Aaron Lukasiewicz.

"Aaron," said the parson, "please sit and unburden yourself of the weight you've carried. Hear your own words. You can't hurt more than you do, and no words can make the pain worse."

The old man hesitated, sat, stared forward and continued.

"I was three or four streets away from ours when the SS car and truck passed me going in the same direction. It turned down our street, and I started to run. I stopped when I reached our corner. They were parked at our building. Officers were at our door already, as the SS troopers jumped from the rear of the truck onto the street and entered our home. I saw it all happening through the falling snow and stood there frozen as it covered my head and shoulders. My father, helpless for the first time in his life, two SS men holding him up by his armpits, appeared at the door. He was shoeless, his stocking feet barely touching the steps and the pavement on the way to the rear of the truck. My mother followed, looking down the street in both directions, looking for me. My wife, carrying our baby, appeared at the door with a woman but no carriage or stroller. They were herded onto the truck, and when they all disappeared into the darkness, the rolled up khaki canvas dropped. Frozen against the wall around the corner, I heard my baby start to scream. I turned the corner, stood there and watched the truck leave. Her screams faded, and so did my need to exist."

He stopped for a moment then continued.

"After everything I loved disappeared, I slid down the wall onto the pavement. The spineless father, son and husband sat there until he was a mound of snow. The next morning the driver of a passing refuse truck noticed the mound moving. The driver offered some hot tea from her thermos. She might as well have dumped me in her bin with the other snow-covered refuse."

The old man started to moan and shake. The parson drew him close until his head nestled against his chest. He fell asleep, exhausted. The parson rose, gently rotated him and set him down prone on the bench with his head on his lap.

Tears streamed down his face as he looked up to a relief of Mary cradling her dead son.

CHAPTER 85

Moe and Diego asked if they could be there when Joseph showed up. He knocked on the locked door at 5 p.m.

Diego tilted the urn and captured the last cup of coffee. Anna sat at the rear table. Moe stood against the counter as Diego started to sort of mop the floor. The Mossad agent approached Moe with his hand extended. In it was the key to Moe's home and the tin with the wax impression.

"This morning we used your key for the last time. All listening devices have been removed. All that remains is our gratitude. Moe took the key and impression, nodded his head in approval. Then Joseph turned to Diego. "We apologize for the discomfort we caused you. We hope you understand."

Diego shrugged it is what it is and handed him the cup of coffee.

Joseph took the coffee and sat opposite Anna. "Mrs. Meir asked us to thank you on her behalf and behalf of all Jews and humanity. You've done all that we've asked you to do. We owe you much."

"Then find me. Find my family," said Anna.

"All we do is hunt Nazis, Anna. We can't help you that way. We don't have the time or budget. For us, time is running out."

"In other words," asked Anna, "You're saying goodbye and good luck?"

"There are agencies we can direct you to. We will insist you become their priority."

"I have no name. No birthplace. No records. What would I ask them to look up or look for? Am I a Jew or a Gypsy or the child of a deceased Nazi buddy? Was I the unwanted daughter of another monster or dead Stormtrooper? Was I kidnapped? Am I the daughter of a partisan they killed or captured or imprisoned? Is my family alive or dead? Where do I start?"

"Mrs. Meir asked me the same question – 'And where does this girl start?' she asked me with that look on her face. Anna, you start with the name of the artist and the date on the back of the cameo you're wearing. He might still be alive. We feel strongly that it was made somewhere in or near Naples because the name is Italian and that's where the cameo carvers are. Show them the one around your neck. Your effort could lead to the person who made it or someone who might have all the answers."

"Just like that? Anna asked rhetorically. "And this is done at my own expense?"

"Again, our prime minister asked the same thing with the same look.

So start there and take someone with you to find this g. Cotto.

El Al will get you to Naples and back first class. We will also arrange and pay for a hotel and give you $40 a day for a week or maybe a little longer if you're on to something. Let us know the dates, the name of the other passenger, and we'll take care of everything else. There'll be a driver named Paolo waiting for you. He's bilingual. He will have a sign that says 'Anna.'"

Joseph rose and looked at the three of them.

"I assume the coffee is on the house," he said. "After you provide the dates, please do not call me again. I'll know if you succeed or fail. Good hunting and God bless you all."

He opened the door and got into a waiting car. Benjamin, in the driver's seat, waved from the window and blew them a kiss. And that was that.

CHAPTER 86

Almost three weeks had passed. Izolda had not been able to use her kitchen table for the entire time. Enlargements of the old man's photographs, books, correspondence, notepads, photostats and scribbles on napkins and envelopes completely covered the table, produced by the indefatigable researcher's efforts "to do the work." The ladies had been all over the phones, library and other sources eager to find what they could use to heal the old man. The name on the street signs and jewelry store set the location. Ceci had been in touch with UNRRA, The United Nations Research and Rehabilitation Agency, and they directed her to The YIVO Holocaust Archives, which had in their possession city lists and ultra-accurate SS records of the deportees, murdered, displaced, missing and survivors. The three rows of numbers tattooed on the old man's arm produced three names, all of which belonged to the same family. Back-tracing indicated they were all transported from Krakow on the same day to Belzec, a labor camp being built nearby. Then, when Auschwitz was completed, the three were shipped there. Auschwitz tattooed their guests unless they were gassed on arrival. The three victims had survived arrival and were tattooed, but within less than a year were ashes.

The names of the three victims were:

Isaac Lukasiewicz nu: 201989

Sarah Lukasiewicz nu: 202266

Ruth Lukasiewicz nu: 202192

The name on the window of the jewelry store was *Lukasiewicz Jewelry*.

The city and hospital records of residents and businesses provided more information. Ruth Solkov married Aaron Lukasiewisz in 1937. The same hospital indicated they had a daughter in 1938. Her name was Rachel.

City business records showed that Isaac and his son, Aaron, became partners in 1936. There was no trace of both Aaron and Rachel on any camp ledger or any list anywhere. The girls learned that more often than not, children, all of whom were considered a burden and nuisance if they survived, didn't make the trip to the camps. Instead, they were trucked to the woods, shot (if they were lucky), and buried. Somehow, someway, their Aaron might not have suffered the same fate.

The four ladies celebrated by going to Jim's Pizza and gorging themselves. They took turns dropping nickels into the juke box selection gadget at their table. Fifties music continued to play for an hour after they left. They made sure of that by dumping more nickels and making the same selection a dozen times before they left the store in hysterics. On the way back to the building Priscilla had asked if she could see the list of tenants. She studied each name until she came to Bella Casper in 1F. The door was open when she got there. Priscilla walked in and there was Bella sewing a karabella together.

Bella looked up and back again. "Didn't you get the rent? I put it in the box."

"Of course we got it. We always do. How are you?"

Other than at night when I'm the only one in my big bed, things are fine thanks to you good women."

"Bella, I have a question to ask you."

"Do you mind if I work while you do you're asking? I spent half a day seam ripping one of your new sewers work of art."

"Bella, is your last name really Casper?

Bella looked up laughing. "Do I look or sound like a *Casper?* The schlemiels sitting behind the bars registering us on Ellis Island couldn't have cared less care about getting our name right. If they couldn't pronounce it they became creative. So *Kasprsak* became *Casper.* Now, I'm almost a Gentile."

On her way back to Izolda's apartment she knew that *Lukasiewicz* had become *Luckman.*

She knew that Aaron Luckman, Isaac and Sarah Lukasiewicz's son, Ruth Lukasiewicz's husband, Rachel Lukasiewicz's father had been listening to Bach in his apartment in the building he saved, four thousand miles from home and their ashes. Priscilla Cates sat down on a stairwell step and started sobbing.

CHAPTER 87

Anna had never been on a plane. Ships, buses, cars and trains were the only transportation she had used. Moe had to tend to his shop and, much to his delight, negotiate a deal with Alphonso Israel who had told him he would retire a bit earlier if Moe paid him a few thousand and took over his lease. Alphonso and his wife of fifty years were headed for Luquillo Beach, Puerto Rico and the mansion he built a few yards from the sand and a few thousand miles from the rotating chickens that paid for it all.

Diego had only been to the city, Connecticut and New Jersey. Bicycle, bus and trains took him where he had to go. He had been very nervous before lift off. A passenger in the waiting area, noticing how fidgety he was, asked if he was nervous about flying. "I have no fear of flying," he responded. "I have a fear of crashing."

Anna was too busy running scenarios through her mind to be nervous, but none of the possibilities were without negatives. None had a happy ending.

The flights to Naples were uneventful and Paolo was waiting at baggage with his "Anna" sign. They stowed no luggage. All each had taken was small back pack duffel. As they left the crowded terminal for the parking lot, Paolo filled them in on who he was and where he came from.

"My name is Paul, but I prefer Paolo. My father is Deputy Mission Chief to Israel. He's Jewish, and so is my mother who was born in the ghetto in Rome. When I was growing up in Hoboken, if my parents wanted the family to have some fun, we would go to Little Italy in the city. We always loved the food and had a great time. When I grew up I asked myself why have fun once a month in Little Italy when I can have fun all the time in big Italy? I went to City College for four years, studied Italian, and after I graduated with my liberal arts degree, collected my graduation gifts and the promised payoff from my father if I graduated and moved to Naples because the best pizza was here. Now I live in Rome but came back here to help you. When I first came here I went to work for company that taught English, but I left for Rome after a few months to start my own business."

"How old are you?" asked Diego.

"Twenty-three," Paolo answered.

"Twenty-three? What kind of business did you start?

"My girlfriend and I put together a two-day course for English-speaking tourists who plan long stays, plan to come to Italy more than once or live here. I teach essential Italian, the dos and don'ts of getting around, buying property and how to maximize the Italian experience.

Even though I'm fluent, they speak a different kind of Italian down here. Their Italian is like their pizza and New York City taxi drivers. It has all kinds of toppings, spices and

short cuts. We'll find who you're looking for, trust me.....
Who are you looking for?"

"Me," answered Anna.

CHAPTER 88

They had walked into the fresh air after Aaron woke up. The sun was disappearing behind the skyscrapers to the west. Lengthening gray shadows from the Hudson to the East River were darkening. The temperature inched down passed comfortable. The parson had convinced Aaron to accept one of his sweaters and walk with him across Central Park West and east along Fifty-Ninth Street to Fifth Avenue. The old man was exhausted but didn't resist.

The parson stopped at the cart of a knish-vendor. "I have this love of knishes," he explained. "My wife cautioned that if I eat too many I might forget that God had a son."

The old man smiled.

The parson continued. "My father taught me that Jews were blasphemers. Alas, I believed that nonsense until my college played against Yeshiva University. My team lost, but I started a relationship with a Yeshiva player whose father was a rabbi. After a few years, I came to the conclusion that Jews were, in fact, the chosen ones, chosen to endure the crap from people who had to blame someone or some group for being miserable and unfulfilled."

They sat on a bench opposite the Pierre.

"Absolution requires contrition, Aaron, but what sin have you committed?"

"The sin of being alive," he answered matter-of-factly.

"Survivor's guilt, my friend?"

"No, Parson, the sin of abandoning the people I loved when they needed me: The sin of not protecting them. I was a coward. I watched them being taken from me and did nothing."

"But Aaron, by 1941 you and the other Jews knew the fate of those Jews ripped away and transported."

"I could have been with them."

"Which one of them?" asked the parson. "How did you know who would go where? The men, women and children were separated. Most likely, your infant child never made the train. You could have done nothing but die with one of them or more likely, alone. You would have been on the truck for a few minutes, been in the same helpless situation you were in at that corner and then separated. Who would they have come home to if one or all of them had survived? Who would be left to mourn, to remember, to teach, to know? Whose heart would they live on in?"

Aaron spoke again. "I started to hunt for them as soon as I could. By 1960 I had all the answers. First they went to a work camp and then one at a time they went to Auschwitz when it was ready and into the new ovens, but not our daughter. The animals took her into the woods with the other children and—"

Before the old man could finish the sentence, the parson lost all the color in his face, grabbed his chest, moaned and fell to the pavement. The old man dropped to his knees, called for help and started to pound the parson's chest. He put his ear to his mouth, and when he didn't hear breathing, bent over, pinched his nose closed and started mouth to mouth until the parson started coughing and he heard the sirens. Two hours later, sitting next to the parson's bed in the Columbia Presbyterian's intensive care's unit, the parson turned toward Aaron.

"Dear friend," he whispered, "the doctor told me that you saved my life. My wife died many years ago. I have no family. Although God is good company, stay with me. Sleep here until you're ready to go home. You saved my life. Give me a chance to save yours."

CHAPTER 89

August in Naples, and the stench of rotting fish, waste from anchored ships in port, from pork, garlic and the annual strike-manufactured piles of garbage on the sidewalks, rendered the city airless and tourists anxious to get to Sorrento and the Amalfi Coast. Dozens of inquiries provided nothing except exquisite street food that made the offerings of the vendors in New York seem like cardboard. Almost everyone in the cameo business knew exactly who *g. cotto* was. He was Giovani Cotto, master carver, who had worked for Cameo Factory De Vito in the city until his disappearance. Over an espresso, a pleasant English-speaking salesman, from the last cameo factory they visited, unleashed a barrage of information about Cotto, cameos, brooches and turquoise. He explained why even the best coveted and hardest turquoise from Iran is too soft, making it almost impossible to survive the carved detail necessary to do a face as magnificent and intricate as the azure-blue one nestled between Anna's collar bones in the hollow at the bottom of her neck.

"Only one carver could have achieved the image that hangs from your neck and everyone in our business knows his story and, with your permission, I'll tell it to you."

"Per favore," said Paolo.

The nice man continued. "Torre del Greco, a town close to here at the foot of Vesuvius was the center of master cameo carving. Giovanni worked with the Scognamiglio family until he left there when Cameo Factory de Vito, a few streets from here, offered him a partnership for a price no one knows.

Cotto had just finished paying in to become a partner when De Vito was caught evading taxes. The De Vitos disappeared with all the money and left Cotto with the disaster, the books and the factory. Then Cotto disappeared and left no trace of the hundred fifty year history of Cameo de Vito and Giovanni Cotto. I hope he doesn't owe you money," said the man as he rose to leave. "He's either dead or hiding from the tax collector in a hill town somewhere in Italy or God knows where. There's no doubt this is his work. He was the only one on this planet who could carve this detail on such soft material."

"Arrivaderci e buona fortuna," he said as he headed away then turned toward them.

"Although he'd be crazy to live in or near Torre del Greco, you should visit Ercolano and Vesuvius. The small city is on the way."

Anna was crushed. Paolo insisted they take the rest of the day off, visit Pompeii and Ercolano and make their last ditch inquiries on the way. They drove south along the coast. Paolo's Fiat sounded like a motorboat. Diego and Anna sat together in the rear. The horrific sights in Ercolano were a much needed distraction for Anna until the present returned along with the fear that unless there was an unknown stone unturned, the chances of finding out who she was were about to go the way of Ercolano that was incinerated by the pyroclastic flow that descended from Vesuvius.

CHAPTER 90

The deal was done. After the city capped the gas line to the window, Moe hired a few men to dismantle and demolish everything. They removed the plumbing, the gas jets and the two rotisserie motors and spits that turned chickens into gold. In one day the space was bare and most of the wall between the old and new space had disappeared. The next day the greasy linoleum was ripped from the floor and the remaining wallpaper removed. Moe spent half the day touring the layouts of the well-known bagel places and delis in the adjoining towns to get some ideas. In a few weeks there would be eight tables of four, an open cooking area on the other side of a display counter and a free-standing glass enclosed rotating multi-shelved unit to display cakes and various desserts.

He ended the day sitting on a folding chair in the center of the new space. His eyes welled up as he spoke.

"Are you proud of me, Sylvia? Are you proud that what was left of your Moe after you went to heaven decided to do more than survive?"

Without checking if the name was available, he ordered a new sign for the shop. It would be called *MOE and SYLVIA'S.*

CHAPTER 91

Ceci had cajoled the Police Station to put out an all-points bulletin describing the old man. After sitting and pacing for an hour she had barged into the captain's office and convinced him to make the effort or face the wrath of the city's 100,000 survivors of the holocaust and 2 million Jews.

On the way out, Captain Mc Crane of Precinct 214 asked her why she made this personal. She answered because she was Jewish. As he looked at her, confused, she said, "I know what you're thinking. We all look the same."

When she returned to the building she found Priscilla and Izolda sitting at the kitchen table, looking down at their cups of cold tea and Rita looking down at a school book and the empty page of a legal pad. Ceci pulled a chair over and joined them. There was no pep talk or small talk. The fear that they had lost the man they had found, the angel who had found them, hung over the four of them.

CHAPTER 92

Torre del Greco was a thriving seaside town twelve kilometers south about halfway between Naples and Pompeii and the road to the crest of Vesuvius. They had decided to go to the crest first and then ask around when they returned, but Paolo and Diego had to relieve themselves before they headed up.

At the intersection of the coast road and the road up Vesuvius was a large piazza filled with shops and restaurants. Paolo drove into it and parked. The men left the car to do their business. Anna remained in the car until it got so hot she had to get out. Next to the restaurant Diego and Paolo had gone into was a shop with some cameos and knickknacks in the window. Next to that was another and another all in a row. She went into shop after shop showing them the cameo front and back. A few of them gave her the thumbs up. A few smiled and said meraviglioso. Anna approached the last store window. One cameo in the window caught her eye. It was the same color as hers. The store keeper, standing in her doorway, watched as Anna held her cameo in her hand and peered at the one in the window.

"Parla Italiano?" asked the woman.

"No, Anna answered.

"Then we'll talk English. May I help you?"

"How I wish you could," she responded.

"Does it have to do with a cameo?"

Anna took the cameo off her neck and handed it to the woman. The woman took the loop around her neck scanned the image and turned it over. She shook her head in awe.

"I knew it was his," she smiled.

"Do you know him?

"I haven't seen him for years," she answered.

Through her tears, Anna managed, "You were my last hope."

"Cara mia," said the lady who took her by the hand, led her into the shop and sat her down.

"Parla con me. Talk to me."

Anna gave her a brief synopsis of why she came to Naples. The lady took it all in and when Anna's story ended, asked her to sit there, and she would be right back.

Paolo and Diego walked into the shop. They heard chards of conversation from the back room.

The shop keeper returned. "Who are these men?

Paolo explained who they were and she relaxed.

"There is no address or telephone. Go up the road about two kilometers. Just before the lava field starts there will be a small dirt trail on the right. Leave your car and these two gentlemen in it. At the end of the trail is a small stone house and someone who might help you. My name is Simonetta. Make sure to call out my name as you near the house.

"But she needs someone to translate," said Paolo

"He speaks perfect English," said Simonetta. "You two pick up some pizza and wait in the car."

Vesuvius was emitting smoke, but it did from time to time. The fiat chugged its way up until the gray, intimidating igneous rock trails and massive stones the volcano had ejected over eons made the landscape uninhabitable. When there was nothing ahead of them except the road through the solemn black lava fields, they slowed up and parked at the trail.

Anna walked the trail until the small stone house appeared. It looked like the houses in fairy tales. As she approached she kept shouting, "Simonetta sent me!"

When she was fifty yards from the house, a bearded man walked through the front door and onto the porch. He was holding a shot gun.

"Chi E!" he shouted.

"I only speak English," she responded.

"Who are you and why are you here?"

"To find out who I am."

"Que?...What?"

She approached holding the cameo toward him.

"I came here to find you because your cameo, if you are Giovanni Cotto, could provide the answers I need to go on living."

He rested the shotgun against the house and beckoned her inside. It was one room that had a few tables including a large work table covered with tools, a pot belly stove, upholstered sofa and works of art including paintings, sculptures and a few display cases filled with cameos made out of coral, turquoise and other materials.

"Simonetta must love you and hate me," he said.

"She is very protective of you, and she doesn't know me well enough to love me. But I know she trusts me."

"Show me the cameo around your neck."

Anna took it off and handed it to him. He looked at the carving, turned it over, and turned it back. He looked at Anna again and didn't take his eyes off of her. She thought she saw tears brimming on his lower lids. He rose, went to a shelf and took one of the dust-covered ledgers to a table. He sat and beckoned Anna join him.

He carefully turned the pages until he found what he was looking for. There was a photo and sketch of a woman inside a yellowed plastic sleeve. He took out both and gazed at them. And then he gazed at Anna again.

"Please turn your head to the right a little."

She did. He looked at the photo and Anna over and over again shaking his head in disbelief.

"Who gave you this?" he asked.

She told them about her Nazi faux parents and he stopped her mid-sentence.

Tell me your name."

"It's Anna," she answered.

"No it isn't," he said. "Your name is Rachel and you are the exact image off your mother. You were born in Krakow, Poland on Kazimierz Street in 1937. A midwife delivered you at home next to your father's and his father's jewelry store because they were afraid to take you and your mother to the hospital after Jewish doctors were prohibited to practice. This cameo was a first anniversary present from your father to your mother. I came to photograph and sketch her and delivered my carving personally to my friend, Aaron. Aaron and Ruth Lukaziewicz were the son and daughter-in-law of Isaac and Sarah Lukaziewicz who did business with my father and grandfather before me. I went there after the war to see if anyone survived. They didn't. The unfriendly Poles who took your home and the business wouldn't talk to me. The records showed your family was taken away to Auschwitz and murdered. I cried the entire flight home to Naples. But now you are here at my table. You are the gift they left behind."

The color drained from Rachel's face and she started to shiver.

"Place your head on the table," said Giovanni Cotto, "and I'll make some tea for the daughter of the woman I couldn't take my eyes off of.

CHAPTER 93

A few days later, Moe, Anna and Diego sat on the sidewalk near the curb on three of the new unboxed chairs watching the new un-grease-splattered window being installed in the new space.

"I think I'd like to do the cooking," Moe thought aloud.

"Did I tell either of you that I used to be a cook?"

"No." Rachel and Diego shook their heads in unison.

"I also ran the deli and appetizing store at the mall in Oceanside."

"So how did you end up here?" asked Diego.

"It happened one morning, a hundred years ago, when I was having breakfast with Sylvia. I was still exhausted from an eighteen hour day in Oceanside. She looked at me, shook her head in disapproval and said, "You work seventy hours a week for a guy who will give the business to his sons, move to Florida, and they will replace you with their cousin or sell it and retire with the cash. Then what?"

"I shrugged I didn't know."

She said, "Putz, you could do the work of three people who you don't have to pay. I'll get a job and we can live from our savings a little bit in the meantime."

"You're telling me to go into my own business?"

"No. You should join the Peace Corp. We'll move to the Congo and weave bagels."

"What if I fail?"

"We put on our bathing suits and swim to Miami."

"And what if we drown?"

"That's the point."

"She must have been some woman." said Rachel.

"Knowing how you turned out, I'm guessing your beautiful mother must have also been some woman," said Moe.

"I know she was special," said Rachel. "And so was my father. Giovanni shared everything he knew about them. Moe, it's the first time I've loved."

"You must be so proud of them and yourself. Let me tell you my plans. I want to have hot breakfast and lunch items and some nice salads. They're putting chicken on Caesar salads. I'll do that too, but I'll make my own croutons. I have space to make bread. I make delicious bread," he added then continued. "I'm not sure about dinner." He took Rachel's hand.

"Someone has to help manage the restaurant."

"What am I, chopped liver?" Diego barged in.

"You're going to graduate school," Moe shot back. "And where did you learn that expression?"

"I heard you say it to the flour guy when you were pissed," he answered.

"Don't be pissed. Keep your grades up, and if I decide to stay open at night, maybe you could manage the dinner shift until you become whatever you decide to become. And what about you, Rachel?"

"Moe, for now I don't know what to do with myself, but at least now there is a 'myself.' I have so much to sort out."

"But it's over, now," said Diego.

"It will never be over, reacted Rachel. The question is what do I do about it?"

A familiar car pulled up behind them.

"Rachel, Benjamin, shouted from the car window, Rachel turned. "How did you know my name?"

"Paolo's father. Come, Joseph wants to talk to you. Come." I'll be back soon," she called out as she headed to the car. Three hours later, she was on an El Al flight to Tel Aviv.

CHAPTER 94

When the parson was out of immediate danger, he was transferred to a regular room. Only relatives were allowed to sleep over. He got nowhere with the head nurse. He asked to see the hospital administrator. The parson shared chards of Aaron's story and their bond with him. The administrator was deeply affected. When the parson was transferred to his own room he found a cot and the administrator waiting for them.

"I'm breaking my own rules because of your incredible story, and in return I want your permission to call my daughter who's trying to make her bones as a staff writer at *The New York Times*. Your story should be read by everyone. Mr. Lukasiewicz, it will educate and inspire millions. And parson, you want to introduce people to God. Your flock could increase five-fold."

"Leave us for now," said the parson. "The two of us will talk and let you know."

"You might go home the day after tomorrow," said the administrator. This will be a perfect, quiet place for an interview tomorrow and for as much time as you need in one of our small lounges. My daughter is—"

Aaron Lukasiewicz interrupted. "I'm tired of judging myself. Let the world judge me. As for me, I think I've at least found peace for now. Tell her to please be here as early as possible."

The old man raced to Riverdale, entered his building and apartment unseen, grabbed his photographs, headed downstairs and out the front door. Rita was standing there, bewildered. Before she could utter a word, he gently put his hand over her mouth and spoke.

"I've been selfish to put all of you through this. Starting today I'm going to try not to be a burden. Be patient, and give the ladies my love. Also, start reading *The New York Times*."

He removed his hand and got in to the waiting cab.

"Jesus Christ Almighty!" Rita screamed after the taxi.

***

The next day, the hospital administrator's daughter sat with her boss, the editor of the Metro Section, the section that featured human interest stories. An hour after her pitch, she sat in room 1104 of The Columbia Presbyterian, her recorder taping their conversation. The next day, the parson left the hospital and returned to his quarters after he invited Aaron to stay with him until the article was printed. After Aaron settled in, the interview continued in Central Park for a few days.

It hit the next Sunday's Metro section. The powerful text caressed the photographs old and new and contained every detail of his life, the good times, bad times, the tragedy, the nightmares, struggle and the relationship with the ladies who each day gave him a reason to stay alive one more.

Rita, Izolda and Ceci and Priscilla holding hands, sat on the floor around Izolda's coffee table. Priscilla sat in an armchair and read the article aloud. Then each read their own copy through their tears. The mystery, helplessness and worry that had permeated their lives were released like the air from punctured balloons. They couldn't wait to see the man who had told the reporter that he loved them all.

CHAPTER 95

Golda Meir, her gray hair back in a bun, looked across her desk at Rachel Lukasiewicz.

"I had to take a good look at you. You're very pretty."

"Thank you, Prime Minister, but I'm sure that's not why I'm here."

"No it isn't. Please sit down, and 1 will read to you an organization's hiring requirements, the personal characteristics necessary to become a member. She read from a printed form:

Candidates must have a diverse set of skills, regularly change identities, live in isolation in distant lands and cope with constant pressure. They must be creative and capable of lying and manipulating others while remaining truthful in their reports. The candidate must have a passion to undo wrongs, expose those who have committed crimes against humanity, follow orders regardless of how difficult or dangerous and must be willing to die for their cause.

Candidates are questioned about all facets of their life and will be interrogated about their personal and

*professional history. Being fluent, including idioms, in two
or more languages is necessary. And then there's courage.
It must be boundless.*

"Rachel, I read your dossier twice. I know your story. That's
why you're here.

CHAPTER 96

Rachel wasn't permitted to contact anyone for any reason. She had called Moe to tell him she was fine and would be away for a while. It was the end of October until she was finished with basic training. There was a knock on her door at five in the morning. Exhausted, she dragged herself to the door and opened it. Joseph and Benjamin standing there, rare smiles on their faces, said, in unison, "Happy Father's Day," as Joseph handed her a copy of *The New York Times* Sunday Metro Section.

When she arrived at JFK, she went to a pay phone.

"Hello Parson Tom. My name is Rachel Lukasiewicz."

CHAPTER 97

Rachel took over two hours to tell him her story.

"Ironic isn't it," said Parson Tom, but the two Nazis who took you probably saved you from being shot, buried or rotting in the ghetto before deportation. They saved you from one hell and escorted you to another. The rest of the Jews in your neighborhood were herded into the ghetto a day or so later."

"Parson, I read my father's story a dozen times. I think I know and understand him, but he doesn't know me. He doesn't know the little girl he sang to sleep is alive. I just can't walk up to him and say, 'I'm your daughter.'" I can't just show up. I don't want to shock him."

"Then come, Rachel. We'll do a little shopping, have lunch and plan the reunion."

CHAPTER 98

Izolda had learned much of what she had to know to maintain the building, and if she was deficient, there was the phone and Ceci. There was also Tito, the handsome Cuban plumber who installed her washer dryer. He looked like Desi Arnaz. Their first kiss sent a shock from her soles to her scalp. Priscilla and Ceci purchased two adjoining coop apartments a few miles from the building. They removed the wall dividing the two, went downtown to find furniture, décor, carpets and what not. They would start and end the day at their new apartment but spend most of their time at the building. Ceci had been on line at Radio City Music Hall to buy tickets for *The Nutcracker*. The gentleman in front of her, holding the hand of his six year-old daughter, was wearing an interesting sort of long shirt. Ceci feigned walking to the front of the line to see why it wasn't moving. On the way back she got a good look at the pleated front of the shirt and the two pockets, one on each side above the hem.

"It's called a guayavera," said the man catching her staring.

"And where can I buy one?"

"You can find plenty in Cuba and never get back here, or go to this one place in Miami."

"One place?" asked Ceci.

"I don't understand that either," he reacted.

"It looks like you can wear it as a shirt or over one. Am I right?"

"Yes, you are right. And you can wear a white guayavera to a baseball game or your wedding."

An hour after the tickets were purchased, the man, his daughter, and Ceci left Wallach's men's store. He was wearing a beautiful oxford button down and carrying his bagged new suit over his shoulder. Ceci carried a bag with the guayavera in it. Shortly after, Ceci's best sewer had it on her table and Ceci was on the phone with Haiti.

CHAPTER 99

Parson Tom told Aaron he had errands to run and hurried to meet Rachel. After lunch, they stopped by an electronics store then headed west to Amsterdam Avenue and up to the West End Synagogue on sixty-ninth. They were there for almost two hours. When they left, the cantor and Rabbi stood in the doorway.

"I wish I was invisible and with them when it happens," said the cantor to the rabbi. Both were weeping.

The parson showed her the bench in the park, handed her the shopping bag he was carrying. Pointing fifty yards away at the men's room, he told her to hang out near there until her father showed up. He then headed back to the church to pick up Aaron and, if he had to, drag him to the park so they could sit and relax.

CHAPTER 100

After Moe received the call from Anna saying she was relocating, he sat there feeling sorry for himself until he understood how lucky he had been that she had entered his life and brought with her the sanitation crew that removed most of the refuse that had littered his mind and had him looking backward instead of forward after Sylvia passed. He wondered what the surprise she promised him could possibly be. He smiled as he stood across the street and gazed at the new *MOE and SYLVIA'S* sign. He now awaited her call to set up an appointment to pick up her things and say her goodbyes in person. He had read the piece in the Times about this old man but didn't put two and two together.

CHAPTER 101

The parson and Aaron entered the park and sat on their bench. After arguing if Tchaikovsky was a bona fide classical composer, the parson rose and said he had to relieve himself. Aaron sat there for a few minutes until a beautiful dark-haired woman in her late thirties sat where the parson had been sitting.

"Dear," said Aaron to the stranger, "my friend was sitting there and he'll be back soon."

"I've come a long way," she said. "May I sit here until he returns?"

"Of course," he answered.

He couldn't take his eyes off her, scanned her face and his heart rate increased. There was something about her.

"Is there anything wrong?" she asked.

He looked away and didn't answer.

"Maybe some music will help."

She took the recorder/cassette player from the bag and hit play.

The cantor's recording of *Oyfn Pripetchik* started.

Aaron Lukasiewicz continued to look away and hummed along for a few bars.

"I used to sing that to my daughter," he murmured, turning toward her.

"And my father used to sit at the foot of my bed and sing it to me every night before I went to sleep," said Rachel.

She moved closer to him, lifted the neck chain and cameo from under her sweater, took his hand and placed it in his palm. They were face to face. He turned it over and back, looked at her.

"I'm told I look just like my mother," she smiled.

"Rachel?" he barely stuttered.

"A Nazi officer and his wife took me before the SS took our family to God knows where. I know they're gone…but… we're not."

They clung to each other and sobbed. No words were spoken until Aaron spoke. "I'm sorry, so sorry I wasn't there for you."

"Papa, I read your story…. I know what happened, but don't you realize that if you had been there for me who would be sitting with me now? Who would I have come home to?"

CHAPTER 102

They spent the rest of the day and most of the night talking, filling in the gaps. In the morning, calls were made to Rockaway and Riverdale to arrange a get together.

After she said "see you soon" to Diego and put the receiver in the cradle, Aaron spoke.

"The men in your life and all the ladies in mine will be there except one," he said. "I want you to meet her."

The ferry was pleasantly empty. As they approached the statue they sat where the old man used to sit. He looked up at her.

"I want you to meet my daughter, Rachel," he said, hugging his daughter to his side.

On the way back, standing at the prow of the ferry, Rachel quipped, "I hope she's not jealous."

CHAPTER 103

There was no small talk during the get together in Aaron's apartment. Questions were asked and all were answered truthfully except one.

"What will you both be doing now?" Rachel was asked more than once. The answer was always the same.

"My father and I are going to Israel. He's going to bear witness and tell his story, and I'll find something to do. Hugs and kisses, laughs and tears, and it was over in a flash. Moe, pushing the reluctant Diego out the door, was the last to leave.

***

Exhausted, Aaron sat at the edge of his bed staring down at his daughter lying there, eyes closed. He sang a verse of the lullaby, kissed her on the forehead, and went to his room. They met each other in the kitchen at two in the morning.

"I dreamed you were gone when I woke up," said the sweat-covered father to his daughter.

"I never fell asleep," said Rachel. "Let's bundle up and go to your summer place, Papa."

He knew exactly what she meant. They dressed. He went to the closet and dug out the blue tarp. Within a few minutes, they were in Van Cortlandt Park in the clearing lying on their backs shoulder to shoulder looking up at the black sky and brilliant stars.

"You know, Rachel, those stars don't exist anymore."

"But we do, Papa. We do."

THE BEGINNING

THE ROCKAWAY BOYS AND MAGGIE

EDITORIAL REVIEWS AND PRAISE

¼ Finalist Amazon's Breakthrough Novel of the Year 2014

Publisher's Weekly Selection.
Glowing CS review 5 Stars 2014

"*The Rockaway Boys and Maggie* can be enjoyed by audiences, both young and old and could easily become an American classic."
—**Red City Review**

"This gang offers us great adventure, but they will also be an inspiration to people of all ages that may be worrying how the new challenges that confront us now will turn out."
—**Five stars Goodreads**

"Thumbs up! The message of the novel is timeless. It chronicles a period in history when New York and America were under attack, but together, the country stood and triumphed–although not without sacrifice."

—**The Wave**

Optioned for film by director, Mark Rydell. 2015

www.ingramcontent.com/pod-product-compliance
Lightning Source LLC
Chambersburg PA
CBHW031943110726
47902CB00001B/276